Usually, I'm a very friendly person. So when Wendy—the new girl in school—needed help fitting in, I decided to change her from a geek to a cool kid. I thought Wendy's makeover would be a breeze. But, boy, was I wrong. The Flamingoes, a bunch of very snobby girls, decided to make Wendy's life miserable . . . so I decided to get even with them!

But before I tell you more about that, let me tell you about my family . . .

Right now there are nine people and a dog living in our house—and for all I know, someone new could move in at any time. There's me, my big sister, D.J., my little sister, Michelle, and my dad, Danny. But that's just the beginning.

Uncle Jesse came first. My dad asked him to come live with us when my mom died, to help take care of me and my sisters.

Back then, Uncle Jesse didn't know much about taking care of three little girls. He was more into rock 'n' roll. So Dad asked his old college buddy, Joey Gladstone, to help out. Joey didn't know anything about kids, either—but it sure was funny watching him learn!

Having Uncle Jesse and Joey around was like

having three dads instead of one! But then something even better happened—Uncle Jesse fell in love. He married Becky Donaldson, Dad's co-host on his TV show, *Wake Up, San Francisco*. Aunt Becky's so nice—she's more like a big sister than an aunt.

Next Uncle Jesse and Aunt Becky had twin baby boys. Their names are Nicky and Alex, and they are adorable!

I love being part of a big family. Still, things can get pretty crazy when you live in such a full house!

FULL HOUSE™: STEPHANIE novels

Phone Call from a Flamingo
The Boy-Oh-Boy Next Door
Twin Troubles
Hip Hop Till You Drop
Here Comes the Brand-New Me
The Secret's Out
Daddy's Not-So-Little Girl
P.S. Friends Forever
Getting Even with the Flamingoes

Available from MINSTREL Books

For orders other than by individual consumers, Minstrel Books grants a discount on the purchase of **10 or more** copies of single titles for special markets or premium use. For further details, please write to the Vice-President of Special Markets, Pocket Books, 1230 Avenue of the Americas, New York, NY 10020.

For information on how individual consumers can place orders, please write to Mail Order Department, Paramount Publishing, 200 Old Tappan Road, Old Tappan, NJ 07675.

FULL HOUSE™
Stephanie

Getting Even with the Flamingoes

Diane Umansky

A Parachute Press Book

A MINSTREL® BOOK

PUBLISHED BY POCKET BOOKS

New York   London   Toronto   Sydney   Tokyo   Singapore

The sale of this book without its cover is unauthorized. If you purchased
this book without a cover, you should be aware that it was reported to
the publisher as "unsold and destroyed." Neither the author nor the publisher has received payment for the sale of this "stripped book."

This book is a work of fiction. Names, characters, places and
incidents are products of the author's imagination or are
used fictitiously. Any resemblance to actual events or locales
or persons, living or dead, is entirely coincidental.

A MINSTREL PAPERBACK *Original*

A Minstrel Book pubished by
POCKET BOOKS, a division of Simon & Schuster Inc.
1230 Avenue of the Americas, New York, NY 10020

A Parachute Press Book
Copyright © 1995 by Warner Bros. Television

FULL HOUSE, characters, names and all related indicia are
trademarks of Warner Bros. Television © 1995.

All rights reserved, including the right to reproduce
this book or portions thereof in any form whatsoever.
For information address Pocket Books, 1230 Avenue
of the Americas, New York, NY 10020

ISBN: 0-671-52273-6

First Minstrel Books printing April 1995

10 9 8 7 6 5 4 3 2 1

A MINSTREL BOOK and colophon are registered trademarks of
Simon & Schuster Inc.

Cover photo by Schultz Photography

Printed in the U.S.A.

CHAPTER
1

◆ ◂ ◆ ◆

"Where *are* they?" Stephanie Tanner said, peering under her bed. "I know I left them here last night." But all she saw was a stack of sketch pads and crayons.

It was Monday morning, and Stephanie had to leave for school any minute. But not without her black leather clogs!

She pulled her head out from under the bed and frantically searched the room.

Footsie pajamas and fuzzy bunny slippers lay on her desk chair. A Monopoly game covered the desk, hotels and money scattered all over. A crumpled T-shirt, a balled-up sweatshirt, and stuffed animals created a small mountain in the middle of the room. Her father would have a fit—he was a total neat freak, and he'd made Stephanie clean the entire room last night before she went to bed. This huge mess had appeared that morning. And none of it was Stephanie's!

"Michelle, you are *such* a slob, Stephanie cried, ready to throw her little sister's stuff in the hall. "If my clogs are under that junk, I'm—"

Suddenly she heard a clomp. A very familiar clomp. The clomp of her clogs!

Eight-year-old Michelle walked into the room, whistling. Stephanie stared at her sister's feet. "*You're* wearing my clogs! I've been looking all over the place for them. Take them off right now!"

Michelle's blue eyes widened. "Sorry, Steph. I was just trying them on," she said, kicking them off.

"Well, try asking first," Stephanie suggested as she slipped her feet into her clogs.

Michelle shrugged, her pigtails bouncing against her shoulders. "I did. I asked Dad. He said to ask you."

Stephanie rolled her eyes. "I don't have time to play around with you," she informed her sister. "And where's my backpack? I can't be late for school."

She started digging through the mountain of clothes. "This place is a wreck," she complained. "And that closet—I haven't seen my cowboy boots for about a year! I can't find anything!"

Michelle pulled her crayons and sketch pad from under Stephanie's bed. "*I* know exactly where my things are," she said proudly.

"Great, Michelle," Stephanie muttered, dashing to the closet to check for her backpack.

Mornings were always pretty crazy at the Tanner house, with seven people and two toddlers trying to wash and shower, get dressed, and eat breakfast. And the fact that Stephanie shared a room with messy Michelle made things even more complicated.

Sometimes I can't stand sharing a room with her, Stephanie thought. *D.J.'s so lucky to have her own room.*

"Hey, Steph, look," Michelle called out. "I drew a picture. It looks just like you."

"Cute. Very cute," Stephanie said distractedly, pawing through the top shelf of the closet.

"You didn't even look," Michelle complained.

Stephanie took a quick glance. She saw a stick

figure with bright yellow hair sticking up all around its head. "It's very nice—but does my hair really look like that?"

Michelle nodded.

"Great, just great," Stephanie said, fumbling deeper into the closet. Her fingers closed around something sticky. "Ick!" she cried, and pulled her hand out of the closet in disgust.

Stuck to the end of her hand was a glob of wacky putty covered with the white fuzz of Michelle's favorite stuffed bear. "Michelle!" she yelled. "How many times do I have to tell you? You can't 'put away' wacky putty by sticking it under the closet shelf!"

Michelle grabbed it. "Thanks, I was wondering where I put that!" she said. "See, you *can* find things."

"Michelle, you're making me crazy," Stephanie exclaimed. And then she saw the clock radio next to her bed—7:59! "Oh, no," she yelped. In five minutes the late bus was leaving. "I'll never make it! Because of you. You and your junk!"

Michelle's lower lip trembled. "You're mean," she said. "I'm not drawing any more pictures of you."

D.J. poked her head into the room. Stephanie's

4

older sister looked perfectly ready for school. Her jeans and matching blue silk shirt were freshly pressed, and her long, dark blond hair was neatly combed. *Naturally—she didn't have to share a room with a slob.*

"What's wrong?" D.J. asked when she saw Michelle pouting.

"Take a look at this place," Stephanie replied. "That's what's wrong. Michelle thinks cleaning up means shoving everything in the room into one big pile. And she's always taking off with my stuff. Like my clogs—and probably my backpack, too."

"I do not have it!" Michelle cried, and ran from the room.

"Oooh! She's impossible!" Stephanie fumed.

"I know," D.J. said. "But she's only eight. You could be a little nicer. I shared a room with you when you were younger, and believe me, it wasn't so easy having you as a little sister. It still isn't. You're in seventh grade and you *still* borrow my stuff without asking."

"Ha-ha," Stephanie called after her sister, who was already walking down the hall. "Not funny."

"What's not funny?" Danny Tanner, the girls'

5

father, stepped into the room. He had a huge mop in his hand and an apron tied around his waist. Usually he'd be at work already, hosting the TV show *Wake Up, San Francisco*. But he had a vacation day today, and he planned to spend it on his favorite pastime—cleaning. He *loved* scrubbing and washing and vacuuming.

"Nothing," Stephanie said angrily.

"Sure doesn't sound like nothing," Danny said, gazing around the room. "Boy, what a mess! Steph, you've got to keep things a little neater in here."

Stephanie glared at her father and said, "I give up."

Danny scratched his head. "Did I say something wrong?" he asked. "It *is* sort of messy in here, isn't it?"

"That's because I live with the biggest mess-maker in the world. I can't even find my backpack!"

"You want me to help you look for it?" Danny asked.

"No thanks," Stephanie said. "That won't solve the problem." She knew what would—getting rid of Michelle! "There's not enough room for me and Michelle in this room, Dad."

"But there will be once we reorganize and redecorate in here," Danny replied. "I'll make sure you have plenty of storage space so we can get rid of all the clutter. I know a thing or two about designing in small spaces, you know. Back in college, Joey and I lived in a room half this size—we had plenty of extra space."

"And we're still best friends," Joey called. He ran down the hall to the bathroom. "I'm next!"

"But, Dad, you've been saying that we're going to redecorate forever, and so far—nothing!" Stephanie protested.

Danny patted his daughter's shoulder and said, "I didn't realize it was this serious. Tell you what, I'll sit down this afternoon and think about some design plans."

"Really?" Stephanie couldn't believe her ears.

"You bet. And," Danny added, "I guarantee that we'll have this room redone within the next two weeks. I swear on my mop." He held the mop handle to his chest.

"Great!" Stephanie couldn't wait to tell Darcy Powell and Allie Taylor, her two best friends. "I'm going to have the coolest room!" Then she yelped, "Oh, no!"

"What?" Danny asked. "You don't like my plan?"

"No," she moaned, "I just saw the clock and I'm going to be late!" She yanked a brush through her blond hair, tossed her denim jacket over her shoulders, and tore downstairs. There, by the front door, was her knapsack, with Michelle's stuffed animals poking out of the top.

Michelle strikes again! she thought. Stephanie dumped the toys on to the carpet, shoved her books into the knapsack, and ran out. She dashed to the bus stop on the corner—just in time to see the late bus pulling away.

Stephanie groaned. *Now I'll have to run all the way to school.*

Ten minutes later Stephanie burst through the doors of the John Muir Middle School. The halls were silent and empty. It was even too late to meet Darcy and Allie. Each morning the three friends met at the pay phone by the gym to catch up. Today she hurried to homeroom and tried to duck in unnoticed. No such luck—not with Mrs. Walker.

"Stephanie Tanner, homeroom is almost

over," Mrs. Walker announced, staring at her over the top of her eyeglasses.

"I know," Stephanie started to explain, "I'm really sorry. But my little sister was wearing my clogs and—"

The bell rang and the students jumped up and raced for the door.

"She took my backpack," Stephanie shouted over the commotion, but no one was listening. She ran for her next class, social studies, and took her seat, pleased to be the first one there— for once. The next few weeks would be really special. Just for their big oral reports, two social studies classes were being combined. Stephanie's class was meeting with Allie and Darcy's for the project.

Allie and Darcy walked in a few minutes later. "Where were you this morning?" Allie asked, sliding into the seat to Stephanie's right. "We waited and waited at the phone."

"The usual," Stephanie replied.

"Michelle and her mess," Allie said, her green eyes full of sympathy.

"You've got to do something about your room situation," Darcy said, perching gracefully atop Stephanie's desk.

"Well, since I can't have my own room," Stephanie said, "I'm doing the next best thing—redecorating the mess out of the room! Dad promised we'd redo it in two weeks."

"Awesome!" Allie and Darcy both squealed.

"And listen—" Stephanie started to say.

"Girls! Please!" came Mr. Cole's voice from the front of the room. "Darcy, I don't believe I assigned you to sit on top of Stephanie Tanner's desk."

The whole class stared as Darcy jumped down and quickly walked to her seat across the room. *How embarrassing*, Stephanie thought.

"And now, class," Mr. Cole said, smiling warmly. "I have a nice surprise for you." He motioned outside, and a second later an unfamiliar girl stepped inside the room. "This is Wendy Gorell," the teacher said, putting his hand on the girl's shoulder. "She's just moved here from Waretown. I know you'll all welcome her to John Muir."

Stephanie eyed the new girl. She was short and thin, with curly brown hair, and a wide, silly grin on her face. But her clothes looked even sillier: a lime-green-and-yellow-plaid skirt that was down to her knees, saddle shoes, and a hot-pink blouse. Her hair was tied up in pigtails with bright yellow bows, the kind Michelle wore.

"Nerd alert," Stephanie whispered to Allie.

"Stephanie, would you like to share what you're saying with the class?" Mr. Cole asked.

"Um, no," Stephanie replied, blushing.

"Wendy, why don't you sit right there?" Mr. Cole pointed to the desk to the left of Stephanie. "Right next to Stephanie Tanner. She can show you around school. I'm sure she'll be very helpful. Won't you?"

"Uh, sure," Stephanie mumbled. She turned to Allie, and the two girls stared at each other with wide eyes and open mouths. A low murmur broke out in the class.

"Settle down, students," Mr. Cole instructed, rapping on his desk with a ruler. "It's time for you to break up into groups. Let's work on your reports on popular culture."

Cool! Stephanie exclaimed, totally excited. Thanks to having combined classes, she and Darcy and Allie would get to do their report together, just like they did everything else together. They had decided on their topic weeks before they'd had to—a day in the life of a fashion photographer. "I bet we have the awesomest idea in the class," Stephanie whispered to Allie.

They were going to spend the day at Darcy's aunt Cece's studio, watching a photo shoot, where real models would be photographed for magazines. There was even the chance that one of them would be discovered and become the next hot supermodel! For sure, tall, slender Darcy with her dark skin, sparkling smile, and big brown eyes would be a great model, Stephanie thought. And so would Allie—

Stephanie gathered up her books and turned to Allie, but Mr. Cole said, "Wait a minute, Stephanie, I'm going to have you team up with Wendy."

"But, Mr. Cole," Stephanie started to say. "Darcy and Allie and I are working together and—"

"That's all right, Stephanie, I'm sure they'll understand." Mr. Cole motioned her to his desk. "It's not easy coming to a new school in the middle of the year," the teacher said in a low voice. "You're such a good student, I know that I can count on you to help Wendy make the transition to John Muir. I'll check back with you in a couple of days to see how everything is going. Okay?"

Not okay, Stephanie thought, nodding miserably. It was her one chance to work with her two best friends! She hated to be singled out like this. It almost made her wish she weren't such a good student. She turned back to the new girl and sighed. What a geek!

Then the teacher said, "Class, you have twenty minutes to write a short paragraph explaining what your topic is and why you chose it. Your reports are due next week. Wednesday. The clock's ticking, so get started!"

Stephanie looked over at Darcy and Allie, but they were already so busy that they didn't even notice her. Glumly she put her books down and turned to Wendy. The new girl gazed at her expectantly.

"It's great we're going to be doing a report together," Wendy said, beaming. "I just know we'll be friends. Golly."

"Yeah. Great," Stephanie said with a definite lack of enthusiasm. "What do you want to do our report on?"

"I have an idea!" Wendy squeaked. "Dolls!

13

We can do our report on dolls! I have an awful lot of them."

"Dolls?" Stephanie asked in surprise. *No way!* "Um, Wendy, I don't think that's exactly what Mr. Cole had in mind. It's supposed to be popular culture. You know, something cool."

Wendy looked confused.

"You know, something hip, or awesome, or radical—like En Vogue,'" Stephanie explained, but the new girl looked even more confused now. *Where was she from, Mars?*

Finally Wendy said, "I think I get it," then flashed another big, goofy grin. "So I'll bring in my doll outfits. I made some of them myself," she bubbled. "And wait till you see my *special* dolls, they're really old."

"That's very nice," Stephanie said, trying to remember the last time she'd picked up a doll—other than the ones Michelle left all over the house.

"We haven't really had any time to figure out what our report *should* be on," Stephanie said slowly. She didn't want to squash the new girl's idea completely. Not yet. "Mr. Cole will understand if we don't give him a topic today. We'll talk to him after class."

The teacher's voice stopped Stephanie. "Who's ready to give their topic sentence?" he asked.

Darcy's and Allie's hands shot up, and the teacher nodded.

They dashed up to the front of the room and eagerly shared their project idea. "We're doing our report on fashion photography," Darcy announced proudly.

"Very nice," Mr. Cole said approvingly. Stephanie stared in misery down at her desk. She still couldn't believe she wasn't doing the report with Darcy and Allie.

"Next?" Mr. Cole looked for volunteers.

Wendy jumped up and shouted, "We're ready!"

"Well, good for you, Stephanie and Wendy."

Stephanie started to protest. "But—but—" But Wendy had already grabbed her hand and was saying, "Come on, Stephie."

Stephie? No one's called me that since I was four, Stephanie thought in growing panic.

"I'm so pleased you're fitting right in, Wendy, thanks to Stephanie," Mr. Cole said as the two girls reached the front of the room.

Stephanie was so shocked, she couldn't speak.

15

She needn't have worried. Wendy spoke for her. "We're doing our report on dolls! I love dolls!"

"Dolls!" Stephanie heard several kids say.

"That's right!" Wendy exclaimed.

Several kids started to giggle. Stephanie felt herself turning bright red. Everyone was staring at her. Staring because they couldn't believe that she'd choose such a nerdy subject. *Dolls!* Even Darcy and Allie were looking at her in horror.

She had to explain that it was all a mistake— a big one—before she was humiliated forever. I . . . uhh . . . well . . ."

At that second the bell rang.

"Dolls it is," Mr. Cole proclaimed. "Class dismissed."

Stephanie was so completely mortified that she grabbed her books and sprinted out of the classroom without saying good-bye to Wendy—or even to Darcy or Allie.

CHAPTER 2

◆ ◀ ■ ◆

There's no way I'll work with Wendy—on dolls or anything else! Stephanie thought as she raced to her next class. *But how could she get out of it?*

"Stephie! Wait up!" came Wendy's high-pitched squeak.

Stephanie sped up, then remembered that Mr. Cole was counting on her to show Wendy around, and slowed down.

The new girl's pigtails shook as she ran to catch up to Stephanie. "Stephie, didn't you hear me calling you?"

"It's Stephanie, not Stephie," she answered

shortly. "I have to get to Spanish class. Where are you going?" *To another school, I hope!*

Wendy pulled what looked like a calculator out of her knapsack and pushed a few buttons. "I have Spanish for second period, too," she announced happily. She punched a few more buttons and read from the miniscreen. "With Ms. Carlton, right?"

"Right," Stephanie answered. "Is that a calculator?"

"Golly, no." Wendy leaned close as if to tell a juicy secret. "It's a digital calendar. Absolutely the latest in high-tech electronics. My whole schedule's in here. It's like a minicomputer. It's got twelve K of memory and . . ."

As Wendy went on about her high-tech toy, Stephanie thought, *Please don't let her be in all my classes!*

No such luck. Wendy was in every one of her morning classes. Worse, she stuck to Stephanie like glue. By English, Stephanie was ready to scream!

Instead of enjoying her favorite subject, Stephanie spent the hour trying to figure out how to show Wendy around as Mr. Cole requested without actually having to talk to the new girl.

She is driving me crazy, Stephanie thought. *And I met her only this morning.*

When the bell signaled the end of Ms. Burns's lecture on the difference between a verb and an adverb, Stephanie sped out of the room. But Wendy was just as quick.

"Hey, Stephie, are you going to show me around school?"

"Um, later. I've got to meet some friends."

"Oh," Wendy said, her goofy grin fading.

Stephanie sighed, remembering Mr. Cole's words. It *was* hard being the new kid. "Come on," she sighed. "I'll give you the Tanner tour."

"Super!" Wendy squealed.

"There's the girls' bathroom," Stephanie pointed out. "The Flamingoes usually take it over between classes. You go through that red door to get to the gym, and that's the health room on the other side of the hall. One of my least favorite places, I might add."

Wendy gazed around in utter bliss, as if Stephanie were showing her a beautiful mansion instead of some ordinary classrooms. "Golly, what a great school," Wendy chirped as they headed down the hall. "It's awfully nice of you to show me everything. Golly."

Stephanie cringed as a group of eighth graders passed by. "Golly?" one of them repeated scornfully. Stephanie tried to move away from Wendy so no one would think they were friends, but the new girl moved even closer to her.

Stephanie sure hoped nobody cool—like Brandon Fallow—would see her with the new girl. And no way was she going to sit with Wendy at lunch.

They rounded the corner to the lunchroom. *Maybe if she didn't talk*, Stephanie thought, *Wendy would get the hint.* But no, Wendy babbled on about her shortwave radio, and how much clearer the signals were in San Francisco, compared to Waretown, where she was from.

"That's really nice," Stephanie said, not having a clue what Wendy was talking about. Electronics wasn't her favorite subject. "Oh, here's the lunchroom. Gotta go!" She dashed through the crowd of kids inside.

I'm free! Stephanie thought happily as she took her place at the end of the long food line. As she waited, she scanned the room casually, as if she weren't looking for anyone in particular, which she was.

Her eyes came to rest on the big round table

to her left, near the cashier. Her heart began to thump wildly. Sitting at that table, with all the really popular guys, was Brandon Fallow, the absolutely cutest guy in the entire ninth grade— and the best forward on the soccer team.

Today Brandon wore faded jeans, a green-and-red-plaid shirt with the sleeves rolled up, and beat-up combat boots.

Stephanie's stomach gurgled with nervousness as she stared. More than anything in the world, she wanted a date with Brandon. Once, she'd almost had a date with him. Well, actually, her visiting pen pal, Kyra, had been the one to date him. But he'd told Kyra that Stephanie was cute. And she was sure that any day now he was going to ask her out.

I wish I could just go over there and talk to Brandon, Stephanie thought. *But I'd probably faint first.*

Then Brandon looked her way. She quickly shifted her gaze to the table behind his, and her smile instantly faded. Jenni Morris and the members of her very snooty club, the Flamingoes, sat there. They didn't like Stephanie very much. And she definitely didn't like them, either.

Stephanie turned toward the back of the room. Four tables beyond Brandon's was the table where she, Darcy, and Allie sat. It was located in a key position—far enough so that Brandon wouldn't hear Stephanie talking about him to Darcy and Allie, but close enough so that she could watch him all through lunch.

She saw her friend Allie frantically waving a chocolate-milk carton back and forth and pointing to it—shorthand for she wanted another, would Stephanie get it?

Stephanie nodded as she thought, *If I ever get through the line.* Sometimes it took forever. By the time it was her turn, her favorite, turkey on whole wheat, was gone. She chose tuna, and headed toward her table.

"Hi, you guys," Stephanie called to her friends, expecting a greeting.

But Allie and Darcy remained silent as their eyes widened and their mouths dropped open.

"What's the matter, do I have something on my face?" she asked, stopping short. "I mean, besides my nose?"

Wham! Someone banged Stephanie from behind, and she banged hard into the table. "Whoa!" she cried, whirling around. "Who—"

Wendy! The girl must have been following her the whole time!

"Golly, sorry I smacked into you like that," Wendy giggled. "I didn't know you would stop so fast."

"How could I tell you? I didn't even know you were behind me," Stephanie snapped. She risked a quick glance at Brandon's table. He probably saw the whole embarrassing episode. But he seemed to be concentrating on some cookies.

And then something even more annoying happened. The new girl pulled up a chair and sat down right next to Allie. "I'm Wendy," she said, "Stephie's friend. Do you know her, too?"

"Stephie who?" Allie asked.

"She means me," Stephanie said wearily as she plunked down on the opposite side of the table. *At least I can see Brandon from here,* she thought.

Darcy wrinkled her nose in confusion. Allie raised her eyebrows and asked, What's going on here?

"Mr. Cole asked me to show Wendy around school," Stephanie explained as she took a big bite of tuna. She sure didn't want Darcy and Allie to think she'd *invited* this nerd to sit with them.

23

Darcy eyed Wendy and said, "That's terrible—"

"—terrific!" Allie cut her off. Stephanie and Darcy could always count on Allie to be very diplomatic.

Stephanie decided to change the subject. "So, did you guys catch *REM Unplugged* on MTV yesterday afternoon?"

"I got to see only one song," Allie said. "Mom had me on garage cleanup duty. She wants to clear out the junk. I guess she's tired of not being able to fit the new car in the garage."

Stephanie giggled as she opened her chocolate-milk carton and took a big gulp. "I should send my Dad over there. He'd have that garage neat, tidy, and *empty* in about ten minutes."

"All the garages on the block!" Darcy kidded.

"Mr. Clean," Allie laughed. "Hey, Stephanie, where's my chocolate milk?"

"Oops, I forgot," Stephanie said. "Sorry."

"No biggie," Allie said as she got up to get one.

"So." Darcy turned to Stephanie. "Are we on for this afternoon?"

"You bet."

"This afternoon?" Wendy piped up. "What's going on? How about you all come to my house and play electronic jacks?"

Electronic jacks? Stephanie thought. She hadn't played *regular* jacks for about ten years.

"Oh, uh, sorry, Wendy," Stephanie said. "But we're going shopping after school." *And you're definitely not invited.*

"Shopping?" Wendy sounded confused, as if she didn't understand why anyone would rather go to the mall than play jacks. "Hmmm. . . . Can I come with you?"

Darcy kicked Stephanie under the table—hard. Stephanie knew exactly what she was thinking: No way!

But how to get out of this one? Stephanie wondered to herself. *Either I hurt her feelings . . . or I have to lie.*

Darcy was practically grinding her shoe into Stephanie's leg now! Stephanie bit her lip nervously. "Gee, Wendy. My aunt is taking us to the mall." She tried to look sincere. "And she can fit only three passengers in her car, max. Sorry."

"But your aunt has a station wagon," said

Allie, who had just returned to the table with her milk.

Stephanie practically choked on her tuna sandwich. "That's, uh, my other aunt, you know, the visiting aunt—"

"But you have only one aunt," Allie persisted.

"Not anymore." Stephanie jumped up before Allie could totally give her away and said, "I really need another chocolate milk." She walked toward the food line. She could feel a hot red flush creeping up her face. *I am the worst liar,* she thought.

"Stephie! Stephie!" her shadow called. "Wait for me."

Stephanie pretended not to hear, but Wendy caught up to her, just as they neared the Flamingoes' table.

She heard Jenni Morris's nasty laugh. "Look at Tanner's new pal," the ninth grader said sarcastically. "Nice pigtails. Maybe *I'll* have to try that hairstyle. On my baby sister!"

The whole table cracked up. Stephanie felt her face turning even redder. Especially because she was sure Brandon heard the whole thing. She didn't dare look his way.

He probably thinks I'm best friends with Wendy.

Jenny and the Flamingoes probably thought they were friends, too. Not that it mattered what they thought. The Flamingoes thought they were the coolest things at John Muir Middle School. The problem was, almost everyone else thought they were supercool, too. Stephanie used to think so—but that was when she was in sixth grade.

She had really wanted to be a member of the Flamingoes. She'd have given anything to wear their pink friendship bracelet, paint her pinkie nail pink like they did, and sit at the Flamingoes' lunch table. Until Stephanie found out firsthand that the Flamingoes were bad news. Jenni had actually tried to trick her into stealing her dad's phone credit card. *Very* bad news.

"Creeps," Stephanie muttered.

"What Stephie?" Wendy asked, totally unaware that half the lunchroom was laughing at her.

"Nothing," Stephanie sighed as she grabbed a container of chocolate milk and headed for the cashier. Her copycat grabbed the same.

"Golly, we are so alike," Wendy said.

If she says golly one more time, I won't be responsible for my actions, Stephanie thought, walking toward the table.

27

As she slid back into her seat, she heard Allie say, "I can't wait till this Saturday!"

"What's going on?" Stephanie asked eagerly.

"You don't remember?" Allie and Darcy stared at her in disbelief.

"Remember what?" Stephanie asked, puzzled.

"The photo shoot for *Sassy* magazine!" Darcy

"And Niki Taylor might be the model! We might meet her. Even interview her. Isn't that totally unbelievable?" Allie exclaimed, her green eyes sparkling.

"Niki Taylor the supermodel?" Stephanie gasped. "I can't wait to meet her!"

"Steph, um, this is for the report," Darcy reminded her.

"Ohhhh." Stephanie's shoulders sagged in disappointment. Her two best friends would be going to the photo shoot without her.

"You could still come to watch, I guess," Allie told her kindly.

"Sure—why not?" Darcy asked.

"Thanks anyway," Stephanie said quickly, not wanting to seem like a bad sport. "But my dad made me and Michelle promise to clear out the junk from our room on Saturday. So, I couldn't come even if I wanted to."

"Oh. Well, that's important, too." Allie smiled.

"Our report will be great, too, Stephie," Wendy said.

Stephanie groaned. "*Please* call me Stephanie. Not Stephie. I hate that!"

"Sorry," Wendy giggled. "So, why don't you come over tomorrow and we work on our report? You'll love my dolls. After, we can listen to my shortwave radio!"

No way! Stephanie thought. "I have a better idea," she said. "Let's split up the work. You do old-fashioned dolls, and I'll research modern ones. Deal?"

"Well, golly, it would be a lot more fun to do it together," Wendy said. "Right, Stephanie?— Stephanie . . . ?" She paused. "What are you staring at?"

"Nothing," Stephanie whispered. *Only the most amazing boy in all of San Francisco.* Brandon Fallow was dumping his lunch tray. Would he look at her? No, he was leaving. Then suddenly Brandon turned around and started walking toward the back of the room.

"He's coming our way," Darcy whispered.

"Ohhh." Stephanie's heart was pumping like a drum as she watched Brandon thread his way through the lunchroom. He was walking right toward their table!

Dimly she heard Wendy insist, "You *are* staring at something. What?"

"He is so completely gorgeous," Stephanie whispered dreamily. "The cutest guy in school."

"He's coming to talk to you!" Darcy nudged Stephanie.

Chill out, Stephanie, she told herself. She wiped her sweaty hands on a napkin. "All right, everybody, act natural. Act normal. Like you're eating lunch or something." She pretended to be sipping from her empty milk carton.

Brandon drew closer . . . closer. . . .

"Well, if you won't tell me, I'll just have to sit next to you to see what's so interesting," Wendy announced. She jumped up—and bumped her tray right into Brandon!

Stephanie gasped in horror at what happened next.

Wendy's half-full milk container flew up into the air and crashed back down hard on her tray. Chocolate milk splattered out of the container— and all over Brandon's thick brown hair and handsome face!

"Hey!" he cried. "What's going on?"

30

Stephanie opened her mouth to say something—anything—but nothing came out.

Wendy's laughter broke the stunned silence. "I'm sorry for laughing, but you do look awful silly with that milk running down your face."

Brandon gave her a dirty look and then turned his gaze on Stephanie. She felt like crawling under the table.

Wendy giggled again, louder. "Doesn't he look silly, Stephie?" Stephanie turned to Darcy and Allie for help, but they were staring at Wendy and Brandon, their mouths open in complete shock.

Wendy must be the biggest geek on the planet, Stephanie thought. *And now I've been humiliated to death.*

With a trembling hand Stephanie grabbed a napkin from her tray and handed it to Brandon. "Are you okay?" she managed to croak.

"Fine, just fine," he said curtly, wiping the milk off his face.

I'll never know if he was going to talk to me. He hates me now, she thought, her heart sinking. *This is the worst thing that has ever happened to me.*

And then Wendy delivered her final blow. "Do you still think he's the cutest guy in school, Stephie?"

CHAPTER
3

◆ ◀ ◢ ◆

"My life is ruined," Stephanie moaned. She was leaning against a sink in the girls' bathroom, where she, Darcy, and Allie had fled after the disaster. "That ... that girl is wrecking everything for me! I'll never be able to face Brandon again."

Her two friends nodded in sympathy. "Wendy *is* a major nerd," Darcy agreed. "But I bet Brandon didn't hear anything she said, especially the part about you thinking he's cute."

"Yeah," Allie chimed in. "He was too busy wiping the milk off his face!"

Stephanie managed a smile. "He did look

pretty funny for such a cool guy." Then her smile faded. "But just the same, I'm never going to set foot in the lunchroom again."

"Stephanie, I'm telling you, Brandon was probably so embarrassed himself that he doesn't even remember you were there," Allie said.

"Besides, how could you live without eating our wonderful school lunches?" Darcy teased.

Despite her misery, Stephanie giggled. She was grateful to have such good friends. They always knew just what to say to make her feel better. But she still wasn't sure if she would go to lunch again.

Just then the door opened and Jenni Morris strutted in, wearing tight faded jeans, a light pink T-shirt, and a dark pink leather jacket. The other Flamingoes followed, wearing pink tops, too.

"Great," Stephanie said, "just what I need."

But Jenni was so busy hogging the mirror that she didn't seem to see Stephanie or her friends. Until she finished admiring her bright pink lipstick. Then she eyed Stephanie through the mirror.

"Where's your new best friend, Tanner?" Jenni

asked snootily. "You know, the head of the geek patrol?"

"I wouldn't know. And she's not my best friend," Stephanie said. "I'm being nice and showing her around."

"Well, don't show her around me." Jenni shot Stephanie a look full of fake pity. "Because her geekiness is obviously contagious!" She let out a nasty laugh, and so did her copycat friends.

"Jenni, you are such a riot," said Diana Rink, one of the phoniest Flamingoes.

"I know. Let's go, girls," Jenni replied confidently. "There are way too many seventh graders in here."

Jenni turned to leave. "Oh, Tanner, by the way, I think Brandon's cute, too," she said.

Stephanie took a short, sharp breath.

"Really cute," Jenni went on. "Just my type, in fact."

"I'm destroyed!" Stephanie cried as the older girls walked out. "The Flamingoes have the biggest mouths in school. If Jenni knows what happened in the lunchroom, that means the whole school knows. Or they will soon."

Allie gave Stephanie a quick hug, her green

eyes soft with concern. "Not true. I think Jenni found a new target—Wendy."

"Anyway, no one with half a brain believes anything Jenni says," Darcy pointed out.

"And she's not too brainy herself," Allie added with a giggle. "Come on, we've got to get to our next classes."

Stephanie walked down the hall to Mr. Spencer's classroom. She took one look inside and groaned. "No! Not *her* again."

The girl who had destroyed her life was seated in the third row—right behind Stephanie's own place.

"Hi!" Wendy said enthusiastically. "Isn't this great? I asked Mr. Spencer if I could sit near you. Hey, why did you leave the lunchroom so fast?"

Stephanie slammed her books down on the desk and stared at Wendy in amazement. "Don't you know what you did to me?"

"What did I do?"

"You completely and totally embarrassed me."

"But how?" Wendy's blank look showed that she didn't have any idea.

The girl is clueless. Totally clueless. "Oh, forget it," Stephanie said, dropping heavily into her seat.

Then Wendy whispered, "Stephanie, want to come over tomorrow after school?"

Stephanie vigorously shook her head no. The girl didn't take the hint. Stephanie didn't want to be her friend!

"Class, I have someone for you to meet," Mr. Spencer announced. "A new student. Some of you may have already met her earlier in the day. But for those who haven't . . . Wendy Gorell, would you like to come up here and tell us a little bit about yourself?"

Wendy practically skipped up the aisle. "Hi!" she exclaimed, a big, goofy smile on her face. "Golly. It's so great to be here. I'm from Ware-town and we just moved. I love my shortwave radio, my dolls, and my poodle."

"Is she for real?" Stephanie heard one of her classmates say.

But Wendy kept on babbling. "My poodle's name is Puffy. He looks really cute when I tie bows in his hair!"

Stephanie groaned silently. How could the new girl act like such a nerd?

"Hey, Wendy, do you paint the dog's finger-nails, too?" Allan Robbins called out.

"Oh, absolutely," she answered seriously.

Giggles filled the room. Stephanie tried to stop herself from laughing, but she couldn't help joining in.

Then came a whisper from Melanie Green in the back of the class. "Weird Wendy, Weird Wendy." Paul Stoneman and Rick Miller picked up it, too. Soon it seemed like half the class was chanting "Weird Wendy, Weird Wendy."

Wendy just stood there, looking confused. Stephanie suddenly felt sorry for Wendy. The poor kid was sure going to have a hard time adjusting to her new school.

" . . . And she just *stood* there, grinning. Admitting that she paints her dog's toenails!"

It was after school the next day, and Darcy, Allie, and Stephanie were headed for Tony's Pizzeria, *the* hangout for the John Muir crowd. It had minijukeboxes at each table, the latest video games, the best pizza—and no adults.

"Hurry up," Darcy urged her friends. "I'm starving."

"So what else is new?" Allie smiled. "Darce, for someone so skinny, you sure pack away a lot of pizza."

"Not just pizza," Stephanie noted. "You pack away a lot of *everything!*"

"So I enjoy my food. Give me a break," Darcy giggled as she picked up the pace.

"Speaking of giving somebody a break, the kids gave Wendy a hard time again today," Stephanie said.

"Well, she is a major nerd," Darcy pointed out.

"And she's a pest," Allie noted.

"That's true," Stephanie said, thinking about how Wendy had stuck to her like glue all day long. "She acts like she's my best friend or something. But how can I tell her I don't want to hang around with her without hurting her feelings?"

"You can't," Darcy said. She pulled open the door to Tony's.

The friends went to the counter and ordered three slices of pizza, plain. Then they made their way through the crowd to their usual booth near the video games. Allie immediately pumped four quarters into the jukebox at their table. "Any requests?"

Stephanie read through the listings. "How about the latest En Vogue song?"

Allie and Darcy both groaned.

"Can't we hear a different group?" Darcy asked.

"Hey—I love En Vogue," Stephanie said defensively.

"Yeah, me, too. But it would be nice to hear someone new for a change," Darcy shot back.

Before Stephanie could reply, Allie said, "Guys, let's compromise. *I'll* pick the song!"

"Okay with me," Darcy said.

"Me, too," Stephanie agreed. She laughed. She and Darcy were best friends, but they sure could argue over stupid things sometimes—like now.

She swiveled around in the booth away from Darcy to check out Tony's. *Yuck*, Jenni Morris and the Flamingoes were in the corner. She turned toward the videos and her stomach lurched. There, standing at the video games, not four feet from her table, was Brandon!

Last time I saw him, milk was dripping down his face, Stephanie thought. *I'm sure he remembers that Wendy said I thought he was cute.* Which meant he knew she liked him. The thought filled her with panic all over again. She whipped back around to her table and whispered, "We've got to get out of here—now!"

"What'd you say?" Allie asked, turning down the volume on the jukebox.

"Oh, yum, here's our pizza," Darcy said as the clerk approached with a tray full of pizza slices.

"We can't stay!" Stephanie insisted.

But Darcy was already reaching for her pizza. "What are you talking about, Tanner?" she asked in confusion. "We just got here. I plan on eating my pizza before I leave. Maybe french fries, too," she said loudly.

"Shhhhh!" Stephanie said, worried that Brandon could hear them. "Brandon . . ." she whispered to her friends.

"Brandon what?" Darcy asked, taking a huge bite out of her slice. She had no clue that he was almost right behind her.

"Not so loud!" Stephanie said.

Allie looked confused. "Why do we have to whisper?"

Stephanie risked a quick look at Brandon. Luckily he was bent over the video game. "Brandon's here. I can't stay. It's too humiliating. He knows I like him, and he hates me!" She slunk down in her chair.

"Will you just chill out and eat!" Darcy said.

"Really, you are acting totally weird," Allie

said. "Personally I think all Brandon remembers is that Wendy gave him a milk bath." She reached for her slice.

"That's what you think." Stephanie grabbed her knapsack. "I'm out of here," she declared. She tried to slip out of the booth, but first she had to climb over Darcy.

She finally got free just as the door to Tony's flew open. In walked Wendy, arm in arm with a gray-haired woman. "This is the pizza place I told you about, Grandma," Wendy said in a loud, cheerful voice.

Her grandmother?! Stephanie thought in horror. Her next thought was even scarier. *If she spots me, she'll try to make me have a slice with her and her grandmother. Humiliation city.* No one over eighteen ever came there. Stephanie quickly dropped back into her booth—right on top of Darcy. "Move over!" she said.

Darcy slid over and teased, "Back so soon?"

"If she sees me . . ." Stephanie said.

"What a nerd," Darcy whispered.

"Wendy has just totally ruined any chance she ever had of being accepted at John Muir," Allie exclaimed. They watched Wendy and her grandmother approach some seventh graders from John Muir.

"Hi. I'm Wendy and I'm new at school," she said, grinning. "This is my grandmother, June. We heard the pizza here was really good."

Before the girls at the table could respond, Jenni Morris shouted from the corner of the room, "Hey, Wendy!"

The new girl's eyes lit up when she saw Jenni. "Oh, hi!"

Jenni gave a loud, mean cackle. "Sorry, Wendy, but you'll have to leave. Didn't you see the No Geeks Allowed sign outside? But your grandmother can stay."

Everyone at Jenni's table burst into giggles.

"That's so mean," Stephanie said, though she had to admit it was sort of funny.

Wendy blinked in confusion and frowned.

"She knows everyone's laughing at her, but she doesn't know why," Allie said in disbelief.

As the three girls watched, Wendy's grandmother patted Wendy tenderly on the shoulder. The two left Tony's.

CHAPTER
4

♦ ◀ ♦ ♦

Wednesday morning, Stephanie, Darcy, and Allie walked toward the school steps together. It was the first time in ages that Stephanie had ridden the early bus with her two best friends.

"Wait!" Stephanie pointed to the top of the steps. A group of Flamingoes was hanging out there, acting as if they owned the place. "Let's stay here until *they* go inside."

"Sure," Allie and Darcy agreed. "So, Steph, did you decide how your room's going to look?" Darcy asked.

"Not yet, but I did tape up some wallpaper swatches to see which colors I like best."

"That's a good start," Allie said.

"I remember when we first moved here and I had to decorate my room," Darcy said. "My mom ended up doing everything. All she let me do was pick out my desk."

"My dad wouldn't do that to me," Stephanie said. "But he does want to talk about his ideas first. They probably have more to do with neatness than decorating, though."

"True, very true," Darcy laughed.

"So, what colors do you have in mind?" Allie asked.

"I'm thinking bright colors. Or, as they say in the decorating world, bold," Stephanie said.

"Bold like that?" Darcy pointed to the bright orange school bus that just pulled up.

"Actually, I had more of a neon orange in mind," Stephanie joked.

"Hire her." Darcy pointed to the stream of kids getting off the bus. Wendy, dressed in neon orange and bright purple, practically glowed. On someone else it would be a look. But on her it just missed. "Talk about bold. You could use her as a flashlight in the middle of the night."

"It's too early in the morning for this," Stephanie said. "Quick—behind the bushes."

The three girls ducked behind the bushes fronting the steps. From her vantage point Stephanie saw that the Flamingoes had spotted Wendy, too. They were pointing at her with their pink-painted pinkies and whispering.

"What are *they* up to?" Allie asked.

"Nothing good, I bet," Stephanie replied, narrowing her eyes at Jenni. *The Flamingoes could be so mean.*

Wendy walked forward, her outfit truly glowing in the morning sun. The Flamingoes' whispers grew louder.

"How weird," Stephanie heard Diana Rink say. "Totally gross," said Paula Stevens, another Flamingo.

When Wendy reached the foot of the stone steps, Jenni bounded down to meet her. She tossed her long, curly brown hair. "Hi, Wen," Jenni said.

Uh-oh, Stephanie thought. *That fake sweet voice means nothing but trouble.*

"So, Wen," Jenni continued, smoothing out an imaginary wrinkle from her tight pink minidress. "Are you coming to my party Saturday night?"

Wendy grinned hesitantly at Jenni. "Golly, I'd love to come to your party, Jenni," she said.

"Where is it?" Jenni turned to the Flamingoes and threw them a big wink.

"Didn't you get the invitation?" Jenni asked.

What is Jenni trying to pull here? Stephanie wondered.

Wendy shook her head.

"You didn't? That's funny," Jenni said in the same sweet voice. "Oops! I must have forgotten to send it. No invitation, no party. Guess you can't come after all."

Wendy smiled uncertainly. "That's okay, Jenni," she said. "Thanks for asking."

Jenni dropped the friendly face and stared at Wendy scornfully. "*Asking?*" she hooted. "She thinks I was inviting her to my party! You don't get it, do you?"

Stephanie's jaw dropped open in horror. How totally rotten!

And Wendy must have felt terrible, too. Because for the first time since Stephanie had known her, Wendy completely lost her goofy grin. With her head down, she shuffled up the steps into the school.

She looks so sad, Stephanie thought. *Maybe she does get it, after all.*

* * *

"So did you find any cool ideas in that *Home Sweet Home* I lent you yesterday?" Allie asked Stephanie during lunch. "My mom says that's *the* best decorating magazine," she added, nibbling at the edges of her tuna fish sandwich.

"There's cool stuff in there. I *think*," Stephanie said.

"What do you mean, *think*?" Allie asked.

Stephanie rolled her eyes. "I can't find the magazine," she admitted. "It's buried in one of Michelle's piles of junk. I swear, if we don't get that room in shape soon, I'm going to lose it. Really lose it."

"Some more shelves would definitely help," Darcy suggested. "Or," she added with a giggle, "maybe you can redecorate Michelle right out of your room."

"Don't I wish, but no way." Stephanie shook her head, her daisy earrings tinkling. "There *is* no other room. But floor-to-ceiling shelves across one whole wall could sure help. Then I'm going to get those awesome miniblinds. Maybe even a walk-in closet. Our little closet is a wreck!"

"Your closet *is* pretty scary," Allie agreed.

Stephanie scooped out a spoonful of raspberry yogurt. "Ooh, listen. It's that new Janet Jackson song. I love it. The Audiovisual Club is finally getting with it."

A few months earlier, the teachers had allowed the club to hook the loudspeaker in the cafeteria up to a radio. The kids could listen to music all through lunch.

"Finally, some decent music," Darcy agreed. "I could listen to this song all day. Hey, here comes the Big W."

"Who?" Allie asked, trying to shove spilled tuna back into her sandwich.

"Wendy," Darcy explained, shaking her head. "Well, you have to admit, it is quite an, er, interesting look. A bright purple jumper and neon-orange turtleneck. With Power Ranger bows in her hair."

"I think she *tries* to look like that," Allie said. "It's on purpose."

"No way!" Stephanie answered. "Oh, I hope she doesn't sit with us again."

"Can't you just tell her not to? You know, nicely, without making her feel bad," Darcy asked.

"I'll tell her tomorrow," Stephanie sighed. Somehow, she didn't feel right about it, with everyone else in the school giving Wendy such a hard time. "She really wants to be my friend." She watched the new girl make her way through the food line. "It's sooo embarrassing!" she groaned.

"It's your lucky day," Darcy said. "She's not coming over here."

"But where else would she sit?"

It looked like Wendy was taking her tray to Jenni Morris's table. But that was impossible!

"That's Flamingo territory!" Darcy exclaimed.

"She's not going to do what I think she's going to do . . . is she?" Allie gasped.

"Oh, yes, she is," Darcy said, her brown eyes wide.

"Didn't she learn her lesson this morning?" Stephanie asked. "Jenni embarrassed her about the fake party in front of everybody."

"Shhhhh!" Darcy craned her neck toward the Flamingoes' table.

"Hi!" Wendy was saying loudly. "Can I sit with you?"

Jenni flashed Wendy a big smile.

I don't trust that smile, Stephanie thought.

"Wendy!" Jenni exclaimed. "Nice to see you. Of course you can, so long as you're a Flamingo."

"Flamingo?" Wendy asked, puzzled.

Jenni laughed. "You heard me. The Flamingoes are the coolest club in the entire school. And *I* am the head Flamingo."

Yeah, Stephanie thought. *The big bird herself.*

"Golly," Wendy said. "I didn't know that."

Jenni pulled the backpack off the chair next to hers. "Of course not. You're new," she said sweetly. "Sit here, next to me." She patted the seat with her pink-painted pinkie.

"Golly, that's great!" Wendy set her tray on the table and started to sit. But as she did, Jenni quickly pulled the chair away.

Boom! Wendy fell to the floor. She sat there for a few stunned seconds, a too-wide smile on her face.

A chorus of laughter rose from the Flamingoes' table. "Oops," Jenni said, "guess you blew your chance."

"That Jenni Morris will stop at nothing!" Stephanie exclaimed. Across the lunchroom Wendy scrambled to her feet and ran toward the door.

"What did Wendy ever do to her?" Stephanie said angrily. "One day someone's going to give that big bird a taste of her own medicine!"

CHAPTER
5

♦ ◀ ◾ ♦

Stephanie had the whole house to herself when she got home from school—for about five seconds. Then Uncle Jesse and Aunt Becky barreled in the front door, each with a twin under one arm and a grocery bag in the other. Nicky and Alex squirmed in their parents' arms.

"Wanna go down," Nicky said, wiggling. "Put me down, Dada," echoed Alex.

Jesse flashed Stephanie a big smile. "Can you help me with my bundles?"

"No prob," Stephanie said, reaching for Alex.

"Actually I meant the groceries." Jesse handed Stephanie his grocery bag.

"Tricked again!" Stephanie complained. Unloading groceries for a house of nine took forever! "I better get some brownies or goodies out of the deal," she said.

"No prob," Becky answered.

Fifteen minutes later Stephanie was still up on the stepladder in the kitchen, stacking boxes of spaghetti in the pantry. "Ten boxes?" she asked. "We'll be eating spaghetti forever!"

"They were on sale," Becky explained. She handed Stephanie the last box. "So what's up? You're pretty quiet."

Stephanie closed the cabinet. "It's this new girl, Wendy. She's mega-weird. Some of the kids are really giving her a hard time."

"Let me guess." Becky smiled. "You want to help her."

Stephanie twirled a strand of blond hair around her finger. "Well, it's sort of complicated," she said. "Wendy really wants to be my friend. Our social studies teacher is making me do a report with her—on dolls! Can you believe it? Like I said, she is a geek. Big-time. She even told Brandon that I think he's cute. Right to his face."

"Major mistake," Aunt Becky said.

Stephanie nodded seriously. "You see what I'm dealing with. I mean, I feel bad for Wendy. I don't want her to get picked on. But I don't want her to think I like her, either. So what do I do?"

Becky pulled a handful of chocolate chip cookies from the cookie jar and tossed one in her mouth. "Mphyspshs," she said, offering the jar to Stephanie.

"Huh?" Stephanie took a handful of cookies.

Becky chewed for a minute. "Sorry," she finally answered. "I was so hungry! That's a tough situation you're in. I remember when the kids in my class made fun of me."

"You?" Stephanie asked in surprise. Becky was perfect. She had the coolest clothes and her hair looked like something out of a shampoo commercial. No way would supersophisticated Becky do anything nerdy.

But Becky nodded. "Yup, back when I was a cheerleader. It was the big Thanksgiving game. It was drizzling, and in the middle of my cartwheel I slipped and fell flat on my face. I had to cheer the rest of the game completely covered with mud. Everyone called me Muddy for about a week."

Stephanie stared at Becky and shook her head. *"That's* your big humiliation? No offense, but that's no big deal. Wendy is being tortured by the Flamingoes."

"Those nasty older girls are at it again, huh?" Becky nodded. "You're right, it's not the same as what Wendy's going through."

"So what do I do?"

"You're a good person, you'll do the right thing." She hugged Stephanie.

"But what *is* the right thing?" Stephanie groaned.

Becky put her hands on Stephanie's shoulders. "I can't tell you what to do. But I know you'll figure it out. And remember this. Sometimes the nerdiest people end up being the coolest. It's funny how that can happen."

"Well, thanks for listening," Stephanie said. She grabbed a few more cookies and headed up to her room. An unpleasant surprise greeted her at the door.

Every single one of Michelle's fifty stuffed bears, dogs, bunnies, and kittens was lined up in rows across the floor!

"Michelle!" Stephanie shouted. There was no

answer. "What is this, stuffed pets on parade?" she muttered.

She tossed the stuffed animals onto Michelle's bed. Then she cleared the crayons and paints off her desk and Stephanie was pleased to finally find the missing *Home Sweet Home* magazine Allie had lent her.

She sat at her clean desk and studied the room, thinking about how to redecorate. In her notebook she wrote:

1) Make the room look bigger.
2) Have more storage space.
3) Get cooler stuff in the room.

She flipped through the magazine, marking the pages she liked with yellow Post-its to show her friends and her father.

At a photo of a red, white, and blue room, Stephanie stopped. Red and white curtains hung at the windows, and the beds were covered with quilts that looked like American flags. She thought it looked cool, but not quite right. *I'd feel like saying the Pledge of Allegiance every morning.*

Then she turned to a picture of a brightly

colored room. But the colors totally clashed. Orange curtains, purple bedspread, and lime-green carpet. Ugh! Stephanie thought. Then she read the caption: *What not to do when you're designing.* As she studied the photo, she realized that the colors were exactly the ones Wendy wore together. *Poor Wendy,* she thought for about the tenth time that day.

Easy ways to double your space, the caption on the next page read. Perfect! The picture showed a high-ceilinged room with two futons laid out as beds, floor-to-ceiling shelves, several hooks extending down from the ceiling, and the coolest blue miniblinds.

She turned the page and saw the same futons folded up into couches, while two bicycles and a pair of skis were hanging from the ceiling hooks. "Awesome!" Stephanie exclaimed. "I could turn this place into a living room!" She placed a Post-it on the page, and suddenly remembered what she was supposed to be working on—her doll report. But what was there to say about dolls? Just that she used to play with them once.

She would work on the report later, she promised herself. *It's not like I owe Wendy—she's not even my friend*, Stephanie thought. After all, Stephanie would have worked really hard on the report with Allie and Darcy. Because, with friends, you cared, and—Suddenly Stephanie sat up straight. *I've got it!* she thought. *I know exactly what to do for Wendy!*

Thursday morning Stephanie rushed to the bus stop. She even beat Allie and Darcy. When they finally joined her, Stephanie cried, "You guys, I have to tell you something. Something very important!"

"Important?" Darcy yawned, and pulled up the collar on her faded blue-jean jacket. "Did you and your dad figure out what to do with your room?"

"Well, I do have some more ideas. But no—"

"So what is it?" Allie interrupted. "Don't tell me—Brandon called you!"

"No! Would you guys listen to me? It's about Wendy."

"Weird Wendy?" Darcy asked in confusion. "What about her? Did she do something geeky again?"

"Come on, Steph, spill it!" Allie added.

They're probably going to think I'm nuts, Stephanie thought. She took a deep breath.

"I have a plan. I'm going to be friends with Weird Wendy," she announced. "I'll make her over so she isn't weird anymore. And," she added importantly, "I think you guys should be friends with her, too."

CHAPTER
6

♦ ◄ ◄ ♦

Darcy's and Allie's mouths dropped open at Stephanie's pronouncement. Finally Darcy said, "You're joking, right?"

"I'm absolutely serious," Stephanie replied, crossing her arms.

Allie stared at her in concern. "Are you feeling all right?"

"Of course I am." Stephanie started to get a little annoyed. She was certain her friends would help her, not give her a hard time. "Are you with me, or not?"

"We're with you. It's just that . . . we're a little shocked," Darcy replied.

"Steph, I don't want to fight about this," Allie said softly. "But you don't even like Wendy. All she's done is embarrass you."

"But if we don't help her, those Flamingoes will think they can get away with *anything*. They'll never stop! Someone has to do something."

"Maybe," Darcy answered. "But does it have to be us?"

"We've had enough trouble with them already," Allie pointed out.

"I don't feel like getting Jenni Morris mad at me!" Darcy declared. "Right, Al?"

"So you think I'm dumb for wanting to help her?" Stephanie asked.

There was a long silence. Finally Allie said, "Steph, we don't think you're dumb. It's just that—"

"Don't worry about it," Stephanie broke in. "Really. I'll help Wendy myself. That's just fine."

The bus pulled up and Stephanie stomped on ahead of her friends. The three rode to school in silence. But as they headed to their lockers, Stephanie tried to explain why she felt the way she did. "You guys, Wendy shouldn't have to suffer just because she's a little different."

"That's true," Darcy said as she fiddled with her combination lock.

"Hey," Allie whispered, "speak of the, um, devil." She motioned to their left.

Wendy had just turned the corner and was walking toward them down the hall, dragging a large paper bag.

Just outside of the math room door, Jenni Morris blocked Wendy's path. "Not so fast," she sneered. Her arms were crossed and there was a nasty look on her face. "Did I say you could walk here, Weird Wendy?"

"Here we go again," Stephanie said.

"Oh, hi, Jenni." Wendy gave an uncertain grin.

"*Hi, Jenni.*" The Flamingo mimicked Wendy's squeaky voice. Then she reached out and gave her a little shove. "Move it, seventh grader."

Wendy lost her grip on the bag. Its contents clattered to the concrete floor. A pair of bright yellow headphones and a jumble of electronic parts fell out.

"And pick up your junk!" Jenni ordered.

Wendy bent to pick everything up, but Jenni started kicking all the electronics pieces around the hall.

"I'm going over there!" Stephanie fumed. "Jenni can't get away with this."

Allie grabbed Stephanie's arm. "Steph, you're just asking for trouble."

"Stay out of it!" Darcy pleaded.

"No way!" Stephanie pulled away.

Just then, Mr. Ryan, the math teacher, stepped outside of his room. He walked right up to Jenni.

"Ms. Morris, what is going on here?" His voice was tight and angry.

"Hi, Mr. Ryan," Jenni said in her phony sweet voice.

Stephanie prayed that the teacher wouldn't fall for it. Jenni had most of the teachers at John Muir totally snowed.

"I'm waiting, Ms. Morris." The teacher tapped his foot.

Wendy was still kneeling on the floor of the hall, trying to organize her belongings.

"I was helping this seventh grader pick up her stuff," Jenni said innocently. "She dropped her bag and everything fell out."

"Good story—except I heard the whole thing," Mr. Ryan snapped. "The way you spoke to this student was disgraceful. And now you're lying to *me*. I'll see you in detention this afternoon!"

"But, Mr. Ryan," Jenni started. "I didn't—"

"And tomorrow afternoon, too," Mr. Ryan interrupted. "In fact, let's make it a whole week of detention." The teacher stalked back into his classroom.

Jenni glared down at Wendy. "You little . . . weirdo!" she growled, her eyes flashing with anger. "You're dead meat, seventh grader. The Flamingoes are going to eat you alive!"

"And so popular taste is influenced by what factors?" Mr. Cole asked during first period social studies class.

"The media?" Darcy said hesitantly.

"Yes!" Mr. Cole answered. As he turned around to write "the media" on the blackboard in big letters, Stephanie flashed a sympathetic smile at Wendy. *There*, Stephanie thought, *that should make her feel better. Especially after her run-in with Jenni.*

Wendy grinned back at her. Two minutes later she tossed a note onto Stephanie's desk.

Dear Stephanie,
    Can we get together after school and work on our report?
    It's due in *six* days!

                                    Your friend,
                                    Wendy Gorell

This is exactly why it's hard to be nice to Wendy, Stephanie thought. *One smile and she thinks we're best friends. But I said I'd help her—and I will.*

As Mr. Cole went on about the influence of the media, Stephanie thought about Wendy. She could really use a friend right now. At least, if she would dress and act halfway normal, she wouldn't stand out anymore.

Stephanie was nice to Wendy during second and third periods, but she still wasn't ready to sit next to her in the lunchroom. As they chose their food and paid the cashier, Stephanie said, "Wendy, I have something I want to talk to Darcy and Allie about in private. I hope you don't mind if I don't sit with you today."

"Golly, that's okay," Wendy said.

Stephanie breathed a sigh of relief and left Wendy standing there, looking for a seat in the crowded room.

But as she sat down, she heard Jenni Morris call out, "Oh, it's the ultrafashionable Wendy, wearing another outfit by those fabulous designers. You know, Gross and Horrible."

"That was so rotten." Stephanie glared at the table of giggling Flamingoes.

"It was rotten," Allie agreed. "But we can't stop them. If we try, the Flamingoes will rank on us, too."

"Wendy may be goofy, but she's not a bad person or anything," Stephanie told them. "When I'm through with her, nobody will pick on her—not even the Flamingoes."

"Not more about your wacky plan?" Allie groaned. "Keep me out of it!"

"Yeah, me, too. Poor, poor Wendy," Darcy joked. "She's about to be clobbered by Hurricane Stephanie. She hits you by surprise—"

"—and takes over everything in her path!" Allie finished. "Like at the talent show, when you wanted to do the choreography, the costumes—*everything!*"

"And I got so mad I almost danced with the Flamingoes!" Darcy giggled.

Boy, they'll never let me forget! Stephanie thought. "Maybe I did get a *little* carried away that time," she admitted. "But we won the contest, right? So give this Wendy thing a chance. I'm absolutely, positively sure it will work."

As she nibbled on her macaroni and cheese, she searched the room for Wendy. The girl sat all alone in a corner. For the first time, she'd lost her air of eager friendliness. Instead, she slumped in her chair, her chin resting on her hand, staring down at her full plate.

As she watched, Wendy began flicking at her hair—and at her shoulders and back. She acted as if a fly were buzzing around her.

At a table nearby, the Flamingoes were laughing hard. Stephanie wondered what they were up to now.

"Now what?" Allie voiced Stephanie's thoughts.

And then Stephanie saw that the Flamingoes had something in their mouths. Straws. They were mashing up little bits of napkin and blowing them—right at Wendy!

"They're shooting spitballs at her!" Darcy cried.

"That's it!" Stephanie slammed her fork down. "I'm saving Wendy—right now."

CHAPTER
7

◆ ◀ ◾ ◆

"Wait!" Darcy cried.

But Stephanie was already striding across the room toward Wendy. The poor girl looked like a scared rabbit as she tried to avoid the Flamingoes' spit-covered missiles.

Stephanie laid her hand on the new girl's shoulder.

"Oh!" Wendy jumped in surprise. She lowered her hands from her face. "Stephanie. You better watch out for the spitballs," she murmured unhappily.

Stephanie grabbed Wendy's hand and pulled her up. "We're out of here," she said firmly. She rushed Wendy right past the Flamingoes, out the door, and into the girls' bathroom.

Tears welled up in Wendy's eyes.

"Hey, it's not so bad," Stephanie said, handing her a wet paper towel.

"It is so," Wendy said miserably. "This school is horrible," she wailed. "I had lots of friends at my old school. I hate it here!"

"Wendy, not *everyone* is mean to you," Stephanie said, although she wasn't sure if that was true.

"But the Flamingoes are." Wendy started crying again.

"You can't let the Flamingoes get to you."

"How do I do that?" Wendy sniffled.

Stephanie swallowed hard. *I have to be honest,* she thought. "Well, you are sort of a little different than what the kids here are used to," Stephanie said slowly.

Wendy's eyes widened. "What do you mean?"

"Well, you act funny sometimes," Stephanie said gently. "I know it shouldn't matter, but it does. As long as you're different, they won't stop picking on you."

"But what do you mean, different?" Wendy looked lost. *Oh, boy,* Stephanie thought, *she has no idea that she's the school weirdo. How do I explain this?*

"Well, um, you act maybe a little *too* friendly," Stephanie said.

"Too friendly?" Wendy looked surprised.

"Like, you don't give kids a chance to decide if they *want* to be your friend or not," Stephanie explained. "And the things you talk about, well, other kids don't talk about that stuff. I mean, like dolls. It makes you seem sort of out of it."

"Out of what?" Wendy asked.

"Like, you're not very cool," Stephanie said as kindly as she could. "You don't talk like the other kids. Or dress like them. Or anything."

Wendy shook her head. "Golly," she said in a stunned whisper. "Everyone liked me at my old school."

"They could like you here, too," Stephanie assured her.

"So what should I do?"

Stephanie smiled. "All you need is to change your style a little bit—a lot!—and learn a few of the expressions we use around here. I'll help you. I've got a plan."

Wendy gave her a trembly smile. "Thanks, Stephanie," she mumbled. "You're really nice."

Well, at least she's not calling me Stephie anymore, Stephanie realized as she smiled back.

That afternoon at four o'clock sharp, D.J. dropped Stephanie off in front of the mall.

Wendy was already there, waiting for her.

Phase one of the Make Wendy Cool program was about to begin. "Did you bring your money?" Stephanie asked.

Wendy nodded happily. "Sure did." She tapped a purple and pink purse hanging at her side. "All the baby-sitting money from my old town. Except what I spent on my shortwave radio."

"Excellent!" Stephanie exclaimed. "Now, first we deal with your clothes and hair. We find you some decent stuff. Then get rid of what you wear and—"

Wendy interrupted. "Get rid of my clothes? I like my clothes. They're cute. And they're comfortable, too."

Stephanie was surprised to hear that she liked them. She figured Wendy's mother had forced them on her. "Well, once you see the awesome stuff at The Connection, you won't want anything else!"

Wendy didn't look so sure. "I don't know . . ." she began.

"Hey, remember what we talked about. Phase one: clothes and hair. Phase two: no more golly! Phase three: music and movie stars."

"Well, if it will make the Flamingoes stop bothering me, I guess I'll do it," Wendy said.

"It will," Stephanie assured her. "By the time I'm done, they won't even recognize you. You'll look awesome!"

"Great—I guess."

"Let's cruise," Stephanie said.

"You're the leader." Wendy saluted.

The girls made their way through the huge mall to The Connection, a trendy discount clothing store. Wendy made a beeline for a rack at the back. "Look, Steph," she squealed. She held up a lime-green-and-purple jump suit with bows at each shoulder. "Golly, I love this!"

"No way!" Stephanie declared. She grabbed the jump suit away and quickly hung it back up. "No offense, but you are clueless when it comes to clothes. Just listen to me, okay?"

"But that jump suit was cute. Especially the little bows."

"Take my advice. Ditch the bows," Stephanie

said matter-of-factly. "And forget about lime green and purple together."

Wendy stared at Stephanie as if she'd just told her the earth was square. "I like that combination."

"Trust me. It clashes," Stephanie said firmly. She pulled Wendy toward the jeans rack, searching for the perfect style.

She finally found a pair of faded blue denim with deep pockets and a loose fit. "Awesome! Try these on while I find some other things for you."

Wendy accepted the jeans hesitantly. "But they're *so* faded," she protested. "It seems dumb to buy clothes that are worn out."

Stephanie stared at her. "Wendy, I know fashion. You don't. Do you want me to help you or not?"

Golly, yes," Wendy said quickly. "I want those Flamingoes to leave me alone."

"Then hit the dressing room," Stephanie ordered. *Boy, if I let Wendy choose what she wanted, she'd end up looking even worse than before*, she thought. She started searching through a rack of oversize T-shirts. She found three: white, black, and red. *Perfect with leggings.* Next she grabbed a few denim miniskirts and carried the goodies to the dressing room.

"I'm back," Stephanie announced. "Let's see the jeans."

"I think they're too big," Wendy said with a puzzled smile. "Look how baggy they are in the legs."

"Perfect!" Stephanie proclaimed.

For the next hour Wendy tried on outfit after outfit while Stephanie made the decisions. She chose black clogs, a pair of black leggings, two T-shirts, a pair of jeans, and a denim miniskirt.

Wendy counted out the cash due—$125—nervously. "Golly," she said. "There goes my new long-life battery pack."

Stephanie laughed. "You and your electronic gizmos. This is much more important."

Their next stop was Accessories, which was filled with sunglasses, hats, scarves, bags, earrings, and barrettes.

"Golly, there's so much stuff in here," Wendy declared, picking up a pair of bright orange sunglasses.

"Try these instead," Stephanie selected round black frames. "They're cool and mysterious— and don't shout Halloween."

At the hair scrunchies Stephanie said, "You've got to get rid of those Power Ranger bows. That's the kind of thing my sister wears—and she's only eight."

Wendy nodded. "But what do I use for my pigtails?"

"Ummm, the pigtails. Did you notice anyone else at John Muir wearing them?"

Wendy sighed. "Nope. So I guess they go, too."

A half hour later Stephanie and Wendy, packages in hand, waited out front for D.J. Wendy wore her brand-new clogs. "These shoes are killing my feet," she complained as D.J. pulled up.

"You'll get used to them," Stephanie promised. She pulled open the car door. "They look totally great." She couldn't wait to get home to show Wendy how to put outfits together.

"Excuse the mess," Stephanie said as the girls entered her bedroom. "I'm redecorating, as if you couldn't tell." She motioned to her side of the room, where different colored wallpaper swatches and pictures of rooms she liked covered the whole wall.

"Golly, it is cute!" Wendy squealed. "I knew

it would be. Look at those adorable posters of the puppies and kittens. I love those."

"Me, too!" Michelle said, marching into the room. "They're mine!"

"Hi, Michelle," Stephanie sighed. "This is my new friend, Wendy. She and I were just about to do something important. Can we get a little privacy?"

Michelle crossed her arms. "I was about to do something important, too," she sniffed. "Give you *my* ideas for the room."

"Go ahead, but make it fast."

"Well, I don't like those little pieces of paper all over the walls," she started to say.

Stephanie giggled. "Michelle, those are *samples*. So we can decide which wallpaper to use for the whole room."

Michelle frowned. "Oh. Well, maybe we could get wallpaper like my posters. Puppies and kittens. And I have another idea," she announced proudly. "Bunk desks. We'll have a lot more room if we put your desk on top of mine!"

Stephanie rolled her eyes. "There is no such thing as bunk desks. And forget about puppy and kitten wallpaper. We'll talk about the room later, okay? Now leave us alone."

"Well," Michelle said, staring up at her sister, "Only if you guys play with me later."

Stephanie knew her sister wouldn't leave unless she agreed, so she nodded.

"I'm outta here, sis," Michelle said.

Stephanie closed the door behind her. "Finally! Now, let's see the new you!" She watched as Wendy tried on the red T-shirt and the black leggings.

Stephanie frowned. "No, don't tuck your T-shirt *into* the leggings," she explained. "Wear it out."

"But it's so big," Wendy said. "Golly."

That word again, Stephanie thought. "Wendy, oversize is the look. And you absolutely have to stop saying *golly*."

"But I grew up saying *golly*."

Stephanie sighed. "Forget *golly*. Repeat these words: awesome, excellent, radical."

"Awesome, excellent, radical," Wendy chanted.

"Now you're getting it," Stephanie cried. "You know, my long black sweater-vest would look excellent with those leggings and that T-shirt. Why don't you borrow it?"

"Well, okay," Wendy said. "If you think I should."

"Sure," Stephanie said generously. "You can borrow my velvet choker, too," she added, opening her closet.

Wendy shrugged, "Okay."

She really appreciates this, Stephanie thought.

"Steph? Are you in there?" Danny called.

"Yeah, Dad, come on in," Stephanie answered.

Danny came in and Stephanie introduced him to Wendy.

"It's always nice to meet a new friend of Stephanie's," he said. "How are the redecorating plans coming? Are my design books helping?"

"I haven't looked at them yet," Stephanie answered with excitement, "but I think a red or bright blue rug—"

"I see pink walls," Danny interrupted. "And flowered curtains. And a toy chest for Michelle's animals."

"That sounds so cute!" Wendy squealed.

Toy chest? Pink walls and curtains? Stephanie winced. "Gee, Dad, I was thinking about something more modern. Like striped wallpaper and futons. Ceiling hooks to hold some stuff. And long shelves for Michelle's animals."

Just then Joey walked into the room. "There you are," he said, throwing an arm around

Danny. "Remember how you were going to help me fix that leak in the bathroom?"

Danny nodded absently, then said to Stephanie, "Honey, I'm sure your ideas are good, but wallpaper can get very dirty. With the special paint I want to buy, you just wipe it clean. And shelves have to be dusted. They're very hard to keep neat and—"

"Uhhh, Danny," Joey interrupted. "I think you'll want to hear this. I decided to prove that I could fix it myself . . ." Joey took a deep breath.

"Why do I feel I won't like what you're going to say next?" Danny mused.

"Well, I started to fix it and the pipe, it . . ."

Just then D.J. burst into the room. "Dad! The leak is turning into a positive flood!"

"I broke the pipe by accident! It was an accident, I swear!" Joey cried. He, Danny, and D.J. raced out.

He wasn't even listening to me, Stephanie thought.

"Boy, you sure have a lot happening here," Wendy said.

"No kidding." Stephanie was kind of upset. "Let's call it a day, Wendy. But promise me you'll wear one of your new outfits tomorrow?"

Wendy hesitated. "What are *you* going to wear, Steph?"

Stephanie pulled a denim miniskirt, a lavender T-shirt, and her black clogs from her closet. Then she grabbed her black-and-white-checked headband.

Stephanie was slipping into her clogs on Friday morning when the doorbell rang. "Steph—" Michelle called out. "There's someone down here who looks just like you."

Just like me? What was Michelle talking about? She ran down the stairs and stopped short. There stood Wendy.

Wendy sure *did* look like Stephanie. She had on the exact same clothes, right down to the black-and-white-checked headband.

Michelle stared. "Did you guys plan this?"

"Definitely not!" Stephanie answered. "Wendy, we can't go to school looking exactly alike."

"But I thought you wanted me to wear what you were wearing." Wendy's face fell.

"Don't worry," Stephanie said. "I'll just throw on my black jeans." She jogged up the stairs. A minute later she was back. "There. That's better," she said, tightening the belt on her jeans.

"Now, let me get a *good* look at you. You look *awesome*."

"Thanks." Wendy smiled. "You look pretty warm."

Michelle looked confused. "Warm? In a T-shirt? That's not very warm," she said.

"She means pretty cool," Stephanie explained. They hurried outside in time to meet Darcy and Allie at the bus stop.

"Nice outfit, Wendy," Allie said.

"Thank Stephanie." Wendy smiled again. "She picked it."

"Even the matching headbands?" Darcy asked.

"Oops." Stephanie pulled off her checked headband. "We don't want to look like twins, do we?"

"I came over wearing almost the same thing as Stephanie," Wendy explained. "But Steph said we couldn't do that. She said people would think it was weird."

"Oh, really?" Darcy asked, raising her eyebrows.

"Yeah, she's really smart about that stuff," Wendy added.

"That's nice, Wendy, really . . . nice," Allie said.

"Steph, that's so *kind* of you," Darcy said sarcastically.

Why are they being so snippy? Stephanie wondered. She turned to Wendy. "Ready for your grand appearance?"

"Yes!" Wendy replied happily. "Thanks to you, Stephanie. You and all your advice."

"I have a bad feeling about this," Stephanie heard Allie whisper to Darcy.

"Hurricane Tanner strikes again," Darcy replied.

CHAPTER

8

♦ ◄ ◆ ♦

On Sunday Stephanie and Wendy had another session in her bedroom. Friday at school the Flamingoes hadn't bothered Wendy at all, so Stephanie felt sure that she was doing the right thing.

"You're almost there," Stephanie declared. Wendy wore black high-top sneakers with bright red laces, a denim miniskirt, and a red T-shirt.

"Cool," D.J. replied. She was helping out, because she had such excellent style. "But this look is crying for a plaid shirt."

Stephanie jumped up. "I know exactly the right one." She dug through her dresser and handed Wendy an oversize red-and-black-plaid shirt. Wendy slipped her arms into the sleeves.

"How about tying it around your waist?" D.J. suggested. "Like so." She tied it around Wendy's waist.

"Excellent!" Stephanie checked the clock next to the bed. In another few minutes Darcy and Allie were coming over and they were going for pizza at Tony's.

D.J. yawned. "Well, gotta go, kids," she said, walking out the door. "I have a date."

Just then the doorbell rang.

"Steph, your fan club is here!" Joey called up the stairs a few seconds later.

Darcy and Allie crowded into the room, in-line skates slung over their shoulders. "Wait till you hear about the model shoot!" Darcy cried. She stopped when she saw Wendy. "Oh, hi Wendy. Nice outfit."

"Very cool," Darcy added.

Wendy grinned and curtsied. "Thanks," she said. "Stephanie picked everything out."

"But of course," Darcy said.

Is she being sarcastic? Stephanie wondered. "I want to hear *everything*," she told her friends, but we're not quite finished here."

Darcy and Allie flopped onto the bed to wait. Allie began thumbing through *YM* magazine. "What do you guys think about Keanu Reeves?" she asked.

"Thumbs up," Darcy said.

"Definitely," Stephanie added.

"Kee . . . what?" Wendy asked. "Is that a thing or a person?"

"A person," Darcy answered. "A very cute person who's been in a huge bunch of movies."

"Oh," Wendy said.

"Don't worry, I'll teach you all about the coolest actors and rock stars," Stephanie proclaimed. From the corner of her eye she saw Darcy and Allie smirk at each other. She ignored them and said, "But first the hair."

She fished through her basket of scrunchies, headbands, and barrettes and told Wendy to sit down. "Now I'll show you how to put this on right. Your hair's sticking up all over the place." She frowned at Wendy's tangled brown hair.

"Oh, show me, too, Steph," Darcy giggled.

"And me!" Allie added.

"Give me a break, you guys." Stephanie turned back to Wendy. "First, you comb your hair back, then you sort of slide the headband on smoothly."

Stephanie watched closely as Wendy carefully obeyed her instructions. "Great! Now poof up your hair in front. And flip the rest behind your shoulders. Excellent!"

Wendy studied her hair and clothes in the closet mirror. "Golly, this stuff just doesn't look right on me."

"Wendy," Stephanie said with a big smile, "you look fabulous. Radical. Doesn't she?"

"Yeah, radical," Darcy mocked. "Her hairstyle's exactly like yours."

"It's true," Allie said.

Stephanie ignored her friends' comments. She turned to Wendy. "Remember what I told you about *golly*? And it's hip-hop music, not hippety-hop. *Rabbits* hippety-hop."

Darcy and Allie rolled their eyes at each other.

"Golly, I mean, excellent. I think. What do I say instead of golly?" Wendy asked in confusion.

"I guess *gee* is okay," Stephanie decided.

"Okay," Wendy said. "Here goes: Gee, I never heard of hip-hop music before. How's that?" She wore a huge, expectant smile as she waited for Stephanie's approval.

"Fine, Wendy." Then Stephanie heard it. Giggles. She whirled around. Darcy lay on the floor, convulsed with laughter. Allie sat on Michelle's bed, holding a hand over her mouth. "Nice, very nice," Stephanie snapped. "What's so funny?"

"I'm sorry, Steph," Allie said, trying to talk through her laughter. "But . . . but . . ."

"Rabbits hippety-hop!" Darcy howled. "Stephanie, you are hysterical. This whole scene is hysterical."

"I guess I don't get the joke," Stephanie said sharply, frowning at them.

"Me, neither," Wendy added with a smile. "But I love jokes. What are you guys laughing about?"

"Nothing," Darcy muttered, getting up from the rug.

Allie got off the bed. "Well, Steph, I think it's time for us to hit the road."

"But what about our plans for pizza "

"That was an hour ago," Darcy answered. "Mom's expecting me home."

"Me, too. I promised I'd rake the yard," Allie added.

"Fine," Stephanie said angrily. "I'll walk you out."

As the three girls walked down the stairs, Darcy sighed. "Don't you think this Wendy thing has gone a little overboard?"

"Not at all," Stephanie said. "Before I got involved, Wendy was the class nerd. Now she's practically normal. I'm really helping her. What's wrong with that?"

"Well," Allie said slowly. "She follows you everywhere."

"She dresses like you, talks like you," Darcy added. "I think it's positively gross!"

Stephanie was trying to do something nice for Wendy. And all her best friends could do was criticize her. "Well, if that's the way you feel, it's a good thing you're not coming to Tony's with us," she sniffed.

"Stephanie, don't be mad," Allie pleaded. "We're just telling you for your own good. We're not trying to make you feel bad."

"I don't feel bad," Stephanie insisted, but as her friends walked out without saying good-bye, she felt a lump forming in her throat. She had to blink back her sudden tears.

Telling herself she had more important things to do than worry about Darcy and Allie, she headed back to her room.

Danny was inside, running a measuring tape along one wall. "Don't you think that's a great idea?" he asked Wendy.

"Golly, I mean, gee. I guess so," she replied hesitantly. "If Stephanie thinks it's a good idea."

"Will I think *what's* a good idea?" Stephanie asked. She watched her father jot down the length of the wall in a tiny notebook.

"To put bunk beds against this wall," her dad explained enthusiastically.

Stephanie bit her lip. She didn't want to make a scene in front of Wendy, and she definitely didn't want to hurt her dad's feelings. *He is trying to help, after all.*

"Dad, I don't think it's what I . . . we want."

Danny let the end of the measuring tape go with a loud *snap*. "Honey, I know *all* about decorating. Trust me, okay?"

Stephanie swallowed hard and said, "Can we talk about it later? Wendy and I are going to Tony's."

Michelle walked into the room. "Hey—it's that girl who looks like you. Stephanie number two." She giggled.

"Very funny," Stephanie said. "I'd like to stay and laugh at your jokes, but we're going out."

"Can I come?" Michelle asked. "I'll tell more jokes."

"Sorry, seventh graders only," Stephanie said. "*Cool* seventh graders. Come on, Wendy. It's pizza time!"

Ten minutes later the girls reached Tony's. Stephanie quickly gave Wendy a few last-minute instructions. "Now, don't order a slice with anything on it. Get plain. That's the coolest. Got it?"

They peeked in the window and Stephanie frowned. That group in pink at the counter couldn't be anyone but the Flamingoes, the last people she wanted to see. A group of guys sat with them. Stephanie hoped Brandon Fallow wasn't one of them.

Suddenly she felt nervous. Stomach-quivering nervous.

But if I turn back now, Wendy will think I'm a big chicken. Some example that would be! I wish Darcy and Allie were here, she thought.

"Ready, Steph?" Wendy's voice broke into her thoughts.

"Absolutely." Stephanie tried to sound confident. She pushed through the door. Everyone in the place looked their way—including Jenni Morris.

"If it isn't Tanner and her puppy dog," Jenni snickered. "She sure seems obedient, Tanner. Woof. Woof."

Wendy hung back, but Stephanie whispered, "Ignore her." She led the way toward the only vacant table, which took them right past the Flamingoes.

As if on command, the Flamingoes jumped up and circled them. Jenni held a piece of pizza crust in her hand. She waved it inches away from Wendy's face. "Here, girl, here, girl," she jeered. "Nice puppy. Tanner's little puppy."

Stephanie saw Wendy's face turn bright pink. Her own face was red with embarrassment and anger. And she couldn't keep quiet for one more second.

"Talk about puppy dogs!" Stephanie fumed. "How about you and your phony Flamingoes? You dress alike, talk alike, you wear your hair the same way—you even wear the same stupid color! You're the ones who follow one another around like puppy dogs!"

Jenni's mouth dropped open in surprise.

Stephanie grabbed Wendy's arm and pulled her back through the pizzeria and out the door.

CHAPTER
9

◆ ◀ ◆ ◆

As she stomped away from Tony's, Stephanie couldn't believe she'd actually told Jenni Morris off. She felt proud of herself. But she felt something else, too.

Fear.

Now I've done it, Stephanie thought. *Those Flamingoes will really be after Wendy—and me, too.*

It didn't help that Wendy didn't say a word. She just walked glumly next to Stephanie, dragging her feet.

Beep, beep! A familiar horn sounded. Stephanie looked up to see Jesse pull his car over. "Hey, what are you two doing?" he shouted out the window.

"Hi, Stephanie," Becky called out.

"Hi, Defanie," the twins babbled cheerfully.

"Want a lift?" Becky offered. "Where are you going?"

Stephanie yanked the car door open. "Out of here."

"Is something wrong?" Becky asked gently.

"It's those Flamingoes," Stephanie said grimly. "They made me so mad, I told them off."

"Yes, and it's all my fault," Wendy moaned. "They hate me. And now they hate Stephanie, too." A tear rolled down her cheek.

Boy, Stephanie thought. *She's even more upset than I am. I have to make her feel better. Whew! This role-model stuff is tough.*

"Wendy, they hated me anyway," Stephanie reassured her. "I've had Flamingo trouble before."

"Wendy, it's not your fault they're teasing you," Becky added. "They're always picking on somebody."

A few more tears trickled down Wendy's cheeks. The twins stared, their lower lips trembling. They hated to see anyone cry.

"No sad, no sad," said Nicky, patting Wendy's hand.

Wendy began to smile. "They are so cute," she said.

"Hey, we're going to the mall to get Jesse some new motorcycle boots," Becky said. "Why don't you guys come?"

"Excellent!" Stephanie brightened.

Wendy frowned. "I'm sick of the mall."

Stephanie eyed her in disbelief. "How can you possibly be sick of the mall?"

Wendy shrugged. "I don't know. I just am."

Stephanie folded her arms. "I get my best fashion ideas window-shopping," she lectured. "And we can check out Smart Stuff and the home-decorating store for my room."

"So, you in or out?" Jesse asked.

"Okay," Wendy said with a sigh. "If Stephanie says so."

"To the mall!" Stephanie commanded from the backseat. "We'll shop till we drop. Browse till we drop, anyway!"

Ten minutes later Stephanie tapped her foot impatiently outside Trudy's Toys and Collectibles. She was eager to get to Smart Stuff, but

Wendy and Becky insisted on gaping at *dolls!* Dozens of them crammed every inch of the store window.

Great, Stephanie thought. *To remind me that I haven't even started on my report yet.*

Wendy grabbed her arm. "Look at that one, Steph!" She pointed at a rag doll that stood two feet tall. It was obviously handmade and very old. "Isn't it the best?"

"It's old and raggedy," Stephanie said.

"Of course it's raggedy," Wendy answered. "It's an antique. That's what I like about it."

"Yeah? Well, excellent doll, Wendy. Ready to go to Smart Stuff?"

But Wendy said, "I have three dolls like that one. They're my favorites."

Stephanie rolled her eyes, but her aunt seemed fascinated. "You have three? That rag doll is special," Becky exclaimed.

Stephanie groaned to herself. Why was Becky so interested?

"Oh!" Becky went on. "Just look at the tiny stitches on the dress. Are your dolls handmade, too?"

Wendy smiled shyly. "Yes. My mom and my

grandmother both make dolls. They make doll clothes, too. So do I."

"Really?" Becky said. "I'm so impressed. Do you think they could show me how to make some?"

"Golly, they . . ." Wendy started to answer, but Stephanie had had enough.

"Hey, guys," Stephanie said importantly. "Are we here to talk dolls or to shop?"

Becky gave Stephanie a sharp look. "Excuse me. I asked Wendy a question."

Stephanie sighed. "Sorry," she mumbled. "But we have an awful lot to do. And the mall closes in an hour."

Becky smiled. "Okay," she said. "But, Wendy, promise you'll tell me more about the dolls later?"

Before Wendy could launch into a speech about her beloved dolls, Stephanie pulled her away. They hurried past the Clothes Line, Archer's Athletics, and the Music Den. They rounded the corner at Yetzel's Pretzels and—

"Ahhh!" Stephanie and her father shrieked in surprise as they bumped right into each other.

"Dad!" Stephanie exclaimed.

"Fancy meeting you here," Danny joked.

"We're hunting for some hip style ideas for Wendy," Stephanie explained. "And some ideas for the room."

"That's great." Danny tried to hide a package behind his back. A big package.

"What *is* that, Dad?" Stephanie asked.

Danny grinned sheepishly. "It was supposed to be a surprise," he admitted. "It's paint for you. Pale pink. Pretty cool, huh?"

"Pink?"

Stephanie thought of the wallpaper samples in her room. Hadn't Danny noticed that none of them were pink?

"I think it'll be perfect," Danny said.

"Pink is okay," she replied. "But I was thinking about striped wallpaper. Remember, Dad? I told you—the day you were measuring stuff in the room."

Danny scratched his head, trying to recall. "I guess I forgot," he admitted. "But I got the paint on sale—it was a great buy! Give it a chance. You'll love pink. I promise."

Stephanie sighed. "We'll see about that, Dad."

"Steph! Steph!" Wendy sped toward Stephanie. It was three o'clock on Monday afternoon.

They were supposed to watch the football team practice. Wendy wore jeans, a turquoise T-shirt, and one of Stephanie's shirts—red-and-black plaid—tied around her shoulders. Her brown hair was held neatly back with a red headband.

"You will never in a trillion years guess what happened!" Wendy said excitedly. "I'm awed!"

"It's awesome," Stephanie said impatiently. She studied Wendy and frowned. "Didn't I say to wear your plaid shirt tied around your *waist?* Not around your shoulders."

And the red plaid with turquoise was kind of a weird match. *But she looks better than she used to,* Stephanie thought. And the Flamingoes hadn't bugged her today, either.

"I guess." Wendy shrugged. "Anyway, Steph, listen. I found a note in my locker."

"A note?"

"Yes," Wendy answered. "From this guy I've seen in the lunchroom. The blond boy who's always with the boy *you* think is so cute—Bobby Zayles."

"Bobby Zayles!" Stephanie screamed. "Sorry," she said, lowering her voice. "He's totally popular," she whispered. "And cute. What did the note say?"

"Wait till you see!" Wendy fished a crumpled piece of paper out of her jeans pocket and handed it over.

Stephanie lowered her eyes and read.

Dear Wendy,

I've seen you around school for a few weeks and I think you're pretty cute. I'd like to take you out for pizza. But the thing is, I'm sort of shy.

Sincerely,
Bobby Zayles

"But he's so popular," Stephanie said, puzzled. "How could he be shy?"

"I don't know," Wendy said, "but he says he is."

"Wait a minute." Stephanie frowned. She smelled something fishy. "Are you sure he wrote the note?"

"Well, I didn't actually see him write it," Wendy said. "But I did see him stop in front of my locker after lunch. And then he passed by a few more times, and each time he stared at me."

"But did he say anything to you?"

"No, he's shy, remember?" Wendy shrugged.

"Anyway, who else would have written that note?"

Stephanie had an idea, but she wasn't about to burst Wendy's bubble. Maybe Bobby really was shy and did like Wendy. Stranger things had happened. "Well, if he *did* write the note, this is your ticket to true coolness," she said.

"Golly! I mean, radical!" Wendy replied.

"And we can find out now, because he's on the football team."

As the two girls hurried to the field, Stephanie wondered what Darcy and Allie would have to say about this. She knew they'd be at the practice, though they hadn't made plans to go together. She was still a little mad at them for making fun of her. And they were acting a little mad at her, too.

She and Wendy climbed up to Darcy and Allie in the seventh row of the bleachers. As they passed by the Flamingoes in the first row, Jenni Morris snickered. *It sure would show up Jenni if Wendy went out with Bobby Zayles*, Stephanie thought.

"He's on the field." Wendy clutched Stephanie's arm as the two sat down in front of Darcy and Allie. Sure enough, Bobby was on the field with the other boys, waiting for practice to begin.

Wendy stood up suddenly. "I'll be back in a minute," she announced, clambering down the bleachers.

Stephanie turned to her friends to tell them the news, but Darcy asked, "How's your little project going?"

"My doll report?" Stephanie felt a stab of guilt. "Oh, I'm going to work on it tonight."

Allie and Darcy raised their eyebrows at each other. "No, your *other* little project," Darcy said.

"Oh, you mean Wendy. Great!" Stephanie replied. "Now that I've transformed her, she's almost cool."

Darcy and Allie groaned.

"You'll see," Stephanie defended herself. "Bobby Zayles even asked her on a date," she added, though she wasn't so sure.

"That's impossible. He goes out with Alyssa Norman," Allie said.

"Well, then why'd he leave a note in Wendy's locker, asking her out?"

"I smell a rat—and her name is Jenni Morris," Darcy said.

A loud burst of laughter rose from where Jenni and her friends were sitting.

"Ohmigosh, look!" Darcy cried.

Stephanie whirled around and saw Wendy headed right for the boys on the football field. "No," she groaned. "She wouldn't go talk to Bobby now." But she did!

Wendy tapped Bobby on the shoulder. Stephanie heard her say loudly, "Hi, Bobby. Thanks so much for your note. It was really sweet. And I'd *love* to go out for pizza with you. When do you want to go?"

Bobby stared at Wendy, a perplexed look on his face. "Note? Pizza?" he asked. "I have a girl-friend. Alyssa Norman. Didn't you know?"

Wendy looked confused. "But . . . but the note. In my locker. You sent it to me."

"What note?" Bobby said with a shrug. "I don't know where your locker is. I don't even know who you are."

CHAPTER
10

♦ ◀ ◢ ♦

The sound of laughter—loud and mean—rang out. Stephanie looked to the first row, where the Flamingoes were howling with glee. Jenni and Alyssa Norman high-fived each other. "She fell for it!" Jenni shrieked. "Weird Wendy fell for it!"

Stephanie couldn't believe that even Jenni Morris could be so cruel.

Out on the field, Wendy's face had turned deathly pale. Slowly she gazed from Bobby to the bleachers where the Flamingoes sat, laughing and pointing.

Stephanie leaped to her feet and shouted,

"Wendy! Wendy!" not caring who knew she was the new girl's friend.

But Wendy stumbled off the football field toward the street. Though Wendy held her hands over her face, Stephanie could tell that she was crying—and crying hard.

"I'm going after her," she told Allie and Darcy, already on her way. As she dashed onto the football field, she shouted for Wendy again, "Wait up!"

No answer.

Stephanie raced after her, but Wendy was so far ahead that there was no way to catch up. She chased her for six blocks, all the way to the Gorell house. Wendy dashed up the stairs of the white brick house, ran inside, and slammed the door. Stephanie was left standing on the sidewalk alone.

Now what? Stephanie took a deep breath and marched right up to the door. She rang the bell.

"Hi, Mrs. Gorell. I'm Stephanie," she said as Wendy's mother came to the door. "I've got to see Wendy."

"Oh, Stephanie," said Mrs. Gorell. "It's nice to finally meet you. Wendy's down in the basement. She seems upset—maybe you can help."

Mrs. Gorell led Stephanie to the basement door. When Stephanie got downstairs, she saw Wendy slumped on a big orange couch, sobbing as if her heart were broken. She barely looked up when Stephanie put a hand on her shoulder.

"Are you okay?" Stephanie asked.

"No! I'm not. And what do you care?" Wendy sniffled. "You think I'm a nerd who can't do anything right. And those Flamingoes didn't do anything to *you*, anyway."

"Wendy, I'm here because I'm your friend," Stephanie said gently, sitting on the couch. "Listen, I've had trouble with the Flamingoes before, remember?"

Wendy raised her eyes, which were puffy from crying.

"Major trouble," Stephanie continued. "Once Jenni tricked me into playing a horrible prank on Allie. It was so awful. Allie ended up telling one of the Flamingoes the name of the guy she liked. The Flamingoes spread it all over school. Allie almost stopped talking to me forever."

Wendy wiped her tears with a tissue. "Golly, Jenni really *is* creepy."

Stephanie sat on the couch and looked into Wendy's eyes. "We're going to make Jenni pay for this," she said firmly. "And when we get her back, she'll never pick on you again."

Stephanie saw a glimmer of hope in Wendy's eyes. "Really? But what can we do to her? She's so popular."

Stephanie racked her brains for an idea. "We could put rotten eggs in her locker," she finally suggested.

"Yeah!" added Wendy, her eyes flashing. "So when she opens it, the eggs will smash on *her!* The smell will last for days!"

Wow, thought Stephanie. *This is a side of Wendy I haven't seen before. She's ready to take action. To really defend herself.*

"How about hiding her clothes during gym class?" Wendy offered. "She'll have to wear her shorts and T-shirt all day!"

"Awesome," Stephanie exclaimed. But then she remembered something. "Jenni usually cuts gym."

"I know!" Wendy cried. "Why don't we glue the pages of her schoolbooks together?"

"Great! Except Jenni wouldn't notice," Stephanie laughed. "Her idea of studying is reading a comic book!" This was starting to be fun.

"If Jenni's such a creep, how come the other Flamingoes follow her around?" Wendy asked.

Stephanie shook her head. "Good question. She thinks she's better than everyone. Even the other Flamingoes. Jenni says rotten things about her own friends behind their backs."

"She talks about the other Flamingoes?" Wendy asked in astonishment. "Let's tell them!"

"I don't think that'll work, Wendy," Stephanie said. "Who will the Flamingoes believe—a couple of seventh graders or ultracool, ultrapopular Jenni Morris?"

"Then we'll have to trick Jenni into saying bad things about the Flamingoes right in front of them."

Stephanie paced the basement floor. "But how?" Suddenly she snapped her fingers and grinned. "I've got it!" she shouted triumphantly. "I'm on the school paper, right? I can pretend to interview her for *The Scribe.* If I ask Jenni the right questions, I know I can get her to talk about her friends. I can tell her I have to tape the interview. Then we can play it back for the Flamingoes."

"That idea's really cold—I mean cool!" Wendy exclaimed.

Stephanie giggled. Wendy was all right once you got to know her.

"But I've got an even better idea," Wendy went on. "See, if she knows she's being taped, she won't say bad things. So why don't you do the interview in the AV studio? I'll run the big tape recorder and Jenni won't even *know* she's being taped."

"You know how to use that?" Stephanie asked.

Wendy smiled. "You're looking at the ex-president of the Waretown AV Club. And I've met most of the kids in the club here. They're nice. They'd let me use the recorder."

Stephanie stared at Wendy in surprise. She thought she was Wendy's only friend.

"So what do you think of my idea?" Wendy asked.

"Really cold," Stephanie said. Wendy cracked up.

"The big question is—how do we get Jenni to do the interview?" Wendy asked.

"Easy," Stephanie replied. "I'll tell her we're doing a 'Who's Cool' issue—profiling the most popular kids. She'll jump at it."

They discussed their plan until Stephanie felt ready to make the call. "I sure hope she's home,"

Stephanie said as Wendy handed her the phone. "And don't make me laugh and blow it!"

Stephanie leaned back on the couch, dialed Jenni's number, and crossed her fingers.

"Hi, Jenni? It's Stephanie. Uh, Stephanie Tanner of *The Scribe*. I'm calling because my editor would like me to interview you for a special issue of the paper."

Stephanie paused for a minute, a smile breaking out on her face. "It's coming out ... oh ... in two weeks or so."

She saw Wendy shaking her head in amazement and holding back laughter.

"In the interview? We'll be talking about *you*, of course." Stephanie pinched herself hard to keep from laughing. "Your thoughts, your ideas, what music you like, that kind of stuff." She turned back to Wendy and winked.

By now Wendy was doubled over in hysterics, her face buried in the couch to keep quiet.

"Shhhh!" Stephanie whispered, laughing a little.

"Think of what your advice will do for people, Jenni," she said. "Oh, did I mention that your picture will be on the front page? Great! Tomorrow, fourth-period lunch. In the AV studio. It will be nice and private."

She hung up, and collapsed on the floor in laughter.

"You were great, Stephanie, just great!" Wendy shrieked as she tried to catch her breath.

When the two were finally able to talk, Stephanie said, "That was a pretty excellent performance, even if I do say so myself."

She pulled her notebook and pen from her knapsack. "Now we need a list of killer questions. They have to make Jenni think the interview is for real *and* get her to diss the other Flamingoes."

For the next half hour the two girls brainstormed. Stephanie wrote the questions down:

1) Where do you shop?
2) What do you think is the coolest thing about you?
3) What are your favorite bands?

"Time to lead Jenni into our trap," Stephanie said.

4) Are you the most popular of the Flamingoes?
5) Why do you think you're so popular?

6) Where would the Flamingoes be without you?

7) Are the other Flamingoes ever jealous of you?

8) Jealous of what? Your looks? Your popularity?

"These are phenomenal!" Stephanie exclaimed. "Jenni is so conceited, she'll make a jerk of herself."

"And then," added Wendy, "we'll make a jerk of her."

As soon as she got home, Stephanie dashed up to her room, lay down on the rug, and started to rehearse her questions for the next day.

"Hi, Steph!" Danny, Joey, and Michelle strolled into the room, their arms full of pink fabric and pink lace. *Yuck, the Flamingo color again.*

"What is that?" Stephanie asked, her stomach tightening.

"Bedspreads and curtains," her dad reported happily. "For the room!"

"For *this* room?"

"You bet." Danny dropped his bundle on the bed.

"Well . . . it's not exactly what I planned," Stephanie said slowly. "Actually it's not at all what I planned."

Danny interrupted her. "But, honey, they'll be so feminine. So frilly. Perfect for this room."

Stephanie shook her head. "Dad, I said I wanted bright colors in here, to liven it up."

Danny folded his arms. "In college Joey and I started out with bright yellow and blue stripes on our walls. We got sick of it after two weeks, didn't we, Joey?"

Joey nodded.

"You won't get sick of pale pink," Danny said firmly. "And besides, Michelle likes it, don't you, honey?"

Michelle nodded. "I love pink," she said.

"Michelle loves bright colors, too. Don't you?" Stephanie said, staring her sister straight in the eye.

Michelle nodded. "I love bright colors," she agreed. "But Dad said pink would be better. He knows, right?"

"Well, Dad, congratulations!" Stephanie exclaimed angrily. "You've talked Michelle into liking *your* ideas! And now I have to live with them!" She stormed out of the room and ran down the stairs into the kitchen. Danny came after her. He paused outside the kitchen door and knocked.

"Mind if I join you?" he asked.

"It's a free kitchen," Stephanie answered.

The look on Danny's face was a little confused. "I know it's hard to share," he began slowly. "But I really think you could try harder. You can work with the pink, you know—add things to make it your own style. Like bright pillows."

"Maybe," Stephanie said. It wasn't exactly what she had in mind. But at least he had used the word *bright*.

"Truce?" Danny asked her. "At least, no more fighting tonight?"

Stephanie had to smile. "Truce," she agreed.

CHAPTER
11

◆ ◀ ▪ ◆

"So, Jenni, what makes you so popular?" Stephanie asked her reflection in the mirror. She'd been practicing since early that morning to make the humiliation of Jenni Morris go perfectly.

"And are the other Flamingoes jealous of you, Jen . . . Jen . . . oh, no!" Stephanie giggled. *How am I going to do this with a straight face?"* she wondered.

"Who are you talking to?" Michelle asked.

"Shhh," Stephanie cautioned. "I'm practicing for something very important." Downstairs, the bell rang. "That's Darcy and Allie," Stephanie exclaimed. She ran downstairs to meet the two girls.

"Where's Wendy?" Allie asked. "Isn't she meeting you today?"

"Wendy went to school early," Stephanie explained. "She had to take care of something. Something big."

"Say!" Darcy demanded.

"It's a long story," Stephanie said. "But I swear you'll find out soon," she added mysteriously. "All I can say is, Jenni Morris is going to learn a lesson."

"That sounds major!" Darcy said.

"It is, and boy, am I nervous."

Stephanie stayed nervous all the way to school and through first period social studies. She kept reviewing the questions for Jenni in her head. And worrying that the tape recorder might break.

Stephanie was so distracted that she didn't even hear Mr. Cole's question. "What was the major population group in northern California during the late nineteenth century? Stephanie, can you answer that?" Mr. Cole said.

"What?" Stephanie asked dreamily. "Oh, flamingoes."

She didn't realize her mistake until she heard the laughter of her classmates.

But Wendy didn't seem nervous at all. *She must have nerves of steel*, Stephanie thought, impressed. Somehow she even made up a convincing reason to be excused early from their third class to set things up in the AV room.

When the bell finally rang for fourth-period lunch, Stephanie's stomach was in an uproar and her palms were clammy and cold. *With good reason*, she thought. *If I blow this, the Flamingoes will make my life miserable—forever.*

Stephanie rushed down the hall into the AV room. It was filled with televisions and video projectors. One wall held speakers and stereo equipment. Wendy and a boy who looked vaguely familiar were working frantically, hooking up red and black wires and fiddling around with screwdrivers and pliers.

"Hi, Steph," Wendy said happily. "Do you know Bill Dunlap? He's in the Club. He's helping out. We'll hide in a minute, as soon as we get the machine all hooked up."

Stephanie nodded at the tall, thin redhead. She didn't really know Bill, but she'd seen him around the halls.

"Oh, no." Wendy frowned. "We have a little

problem. The positive cord shorted out, so we have to splice a new one."

"Shorted out?" Stephanie gasped, her voice squeaking in panic. "Splice? What are you talking about?" She looked at her watch. Jenni was due in five minutes!

"Golly, I'll explain later," Wendy said distractedly. "Hit the DEF switch while I make sure it's positive-positive and negative-negative," she told Bill.

"Positively," Bill replied.

Wow, Stephanie thought, *she really knows this electronics stuff.*

Stephanie looked at her watch—12:09! Jenni was due in one minute! "Hurry!" she urged.

"There!" Wendy said triumphantly. "We got it."

Relief washed over Stephanie. "You better hide, quick!"

Wendy and Bill disappeared behind a speaker at the back of the studio. "Remember," Wendy said, "wait until I give you the thumbs-up signal. That means the tape is rolling."

She ducked back down just as Jenni walked in, her pink combat boots clomping loudly on the tile floor. *There is no way my room is going to be pink*, Stephanie thought.

"Hello, Jenni." Stephanie offered her a chair. "I'd like to thank you for agreeing to this interview. I think it will be truly fascinating for our readers."

Truly fascinating for the Flamingoes, Stephanie thought.

Jenni rolled her eyes. "Cut it, Tanner," she said. "You have twenty minutes. Then I've got to get back to the lunchroom for a special Flamingoes meeting."

Well, excuuuuuse me, Stephanie thought, sitting in a chair facing Jenni. She peered at the end of the room where Wendy and Bill hid. No signal, yet.

I've got to stall her, Stephanie thought. "Jenni," she squealed. "That is the most radical uh . . . T-shirt I've ever seen." Jenni *always* fell for flattery.

"It is pretty excellent," Jenni said. "But I have about ten others that are just as cool."

"I'm sure you do," Stephanie said sweetly. "You have the best clothes." *Where was that sign?*

Finally Wendy's thumb poked up from behind the speaker.

"In fact," Stephanie said quickly. "That was going to be my first question. How do you put together such a fabulous wardrobe?"

As Jenni droned on about her strong sense of color and style, Stephanie pretended to be taking notes. What she was actually writing over and over again on her pad was "Jenni Morris is a big, stuck-up snob."

After style, Jenni talked about hair, makeup, and her nails. "I use a cuticle cream once a day," she confided.

She is really boring, Stephanie thought in surprise. "Jenni, what makes you so popular?" she asked.

"A lot of things," Jenni answered. "My looks, my personality, my leadership ability—"

Stephanie moved in for the kill. "You are definitely the most popular girl in school. Are the other Flamingoes ever jealous?"

"It is a problem," Jenni admitted. "I don't want to make the other Flamingoes feel bad. But it's hard because I am so popular. And let's face it, I'm the prettiest."

Whew! And the most conceited, Stephanie thought.

"Does that ever cause, er, dating problems?" Stephanie asked.

"Does it!" Jenni exploded. "All the guys in school like me, even the guys the other Flamingoes are interested in. I could date *any* guy. But I have to leave something for the other Flamingoes."

That tape recorder better be working, Stephanie thought as she asked her final question. "Do the other Flamingoes try to copy you?"

"They all copy me—my clothes, my hair, the way I talk," Jenni shot back. "They're always begging to borrow my clothes. It gets so boring. But I guess that's what I have to put up with as the leader. I mean, if it wasn't for me, there wouldn't even be any Flamingoes. I *am* the Flamingoes!"

Stephanie finished writing. "A really big snob and a jerk" were the last notes on her pad. "That was an excellent interview," she said. "I think you'll be very surprised at the reaction you get."

"Surprised?" Jenni asked, standing up. She wrinkled her brow. "Tanner, you won't use any of the stuff I said about the other Flamingoes, will you? I mean, you better not."

Stephanie stood up. "Jenni, I promise you that

none of your criticisms of the Flamingoes will appear in *The Scribe*."

And I'm not lying, either, Stephanie thought. *There's no way that anything Jenni Morris said will end up in The Scribe.*

The moment Jenni walked out, Wendy and Bill sprang from their hiding place. "We did it! We did it!" they yelled, high-fiving each other. Stephanie hugged Wendy. "I can't believe we got Jenni Morris to say all those mega-conceited things on tape."

"You were great, Steph." Wendy giggled. "I couldn't believe those answers of hers. Talk about mean!"

Stephanie grinned. "I wonder how many Flamingoes will still be in the club once they hear our little recording?"

"They won't have to wait to hear the tape recording," Wendy said with a mysterious smile.

"What are you talking about?" Stephanie asked.

Wendy grinned from ear to ear, looking as if she were ready to explode, but all she said was, "Wait until you find out what we did. It's so awesome. The big Flamingo will be a dead duck!"

CHAPTER
12

◆ ◢ ◣ ◆

"Dead duck? What do you mean?" Stephanie asked, confused.

"Come on and you'll see," Wendy said, already pulling Stephanie out the door. "I think you're going to enjoy lunch today. *Really* enjoy it."

"Why? Are they serving Tony's pizza?" Stephanie joked.

"Something better." Wendy pushed open the lunchroom door.

"Wow!" Stephanie exclaimed. The lunchroom was noisier than ever. *Much* noisier. And kids all over the room kept repeating the name Jenni Morris.

"Something's up." Stephanie glanced at the Flamingoes. She couldn't believe her eyes. Usually, they sat around looking cool and making fun of the seventh graders that dared to walk by their table. But today they stood in a circle around the table. And they definitely didn't look cool. They looked *mad*.

And the object of their anger was none other than—Jenni Morris! The big bird sat at the table with a stunned expression.

"She looks like she's ready to cry," Stephanie said, in total shock.

"Come on." Wendy pulled her forward. "Let's go on the food line so we can hear what they're saying."

The Flamingoes were yelling. Yelling at Jenni!

"Let me get this straight, you're so popular that you could get any guy in school?" Diana Rink shouted.

"And we're all jealous of you? Is that what you think, Jenni Morris?" snapped Tina Brewer.

Jenni gazed up at her friends with a pleading look. "No," she said. "Come on, you know I'd never say anything like that."

"Hah!" Diana Rink snorted.

"Diana, please," Jenni begged. "You've got to believe me."

"Is somebody talking to me?" Diana said angrily, pretending she didn't hear Jenni. She sat down, turning her back to Jenni. The other Flamingoes did the same.

Jenni Morris, the big leader of the Flamingoes, was faced with a wall of backs.

"Unbelievable!" Stephanie exclaimed. "But what happened? They already know what's on the tape."

Before Wendy could answer, Jenni jumped up and ran over to Stephanie, her features twisted in anger. "You!" she screamed. "What did you do?"

"I interviewed you," Stephanie said, stepping back.

"You promised you wouldn't tell the Flamingoes what I said. And how did you tell them so fast?"

How did we? Stephanie wondered. She grabbed Wendy's arm for support. The new girl chuckled.

"Anything wrong, Jenni?" Wendy asked. She stared directly at Jenni, not a hint of fear on her face.

"What kind of lousy trick did you play on me,

Weird Wendy?" Jenni demanded. "What did you tell the Flamingoes?"

The room grew suddenly quiet. It seemed everyone was waiting for Wendy's answer.

The new girl calmly explained herself. "We didn't tell the Flamingoes anything. *You* did that. Bill and I were in the AV studio during the interview. You know, where the lunchroom music comes from. Well, we hooked things up so that instead of music, your interview was broadcast over the speakers in the lunchroom. How could we know you'd be so nasty?"

Stephanie saw that all the kids were staring at Wendy in amazement. "What guts!" someone called out. "Good going!"

Jenni's mouth dropped open. "How dare you?" she spluttered at Wendy and Stephanie. "You betrayed me!"

"You did that yourself," Wendy replied. "*You* did the talking. Maybe next time you won't be so mean."

"Yeah, Jenni," Stephanie added. "Everyone around here is sick of your mean tricks. Now you know how it feels!"

"All right, Wendy!" a cheer rose from the seventh grade side of the room.

Wendy wasn't the new girl any longer—she was the cool girl!

"You'll pay for this, Weird Wendy!" Jenni promised. "You, too, Tanner." She turned on her heel and stalked out.

The lunchroom exploded with laughter and cheers.

Darcy and Allie ran over to the trio. "Way to go!"

"Wow!" Darcy exclaimed. "That was so great, seeing Jenni Morris get a dose of her own meanness."

"How'd you do it?" Allie asked.

Wendy explained as more and more kids came up to congratulate her and Stephanie. "What a day," she said happily. "Golly!"

Stephanie groaned. "Wendy, I can't believe you said that word again."

Wendy's smile disappeared instantly. "I hate to say this, Stephanie—but I'm tired of your trying to run my life!"

CHAPTER
13

◆ ◢ ◼ ◆

Stephanie stared in shock as Wendy stalked off to another table. The kids instantly made room for her. "I taught her how to dress, to act, do her hair. I can't believe she's mad at me for one little comment."

Darcy and Allie exchanged glances.

"Maybe Wendy is right," Darcy said carefully.

"What exactly do you mean?" Stephanie asked.

Allie hesitated. "You haven't been trying to help Wendy be herself. You've been trying to turn her into another Stephanie. And you have to admit, getting even with Jenni was as much for you as it was for Wendy."

Stephanie felt like she'd been punched in the stomach. "I have not tried to make her into me!" she said hotly. "I tried to help Wendy. You guys just made fun of her." She glared at her friends.

"We're just trying to be honest with you, Steph," Darcy said. "You have been pretty bossy with Wendy. And not much fun to be around lately."

Stephanie was so mad that she dumped her full tray into the Dumpster. "Well, *thank you* for being honest!" she sputtered. "It's nice to know that my best friends think I'm bossy. You're probably *glad* I'm not doing my social studies report with you. I'd just take over, wouldn't I?"

The bell rang and Stephanie whirled toward the lunchroom door. "Don't bother calling me later!" she said angrily. "I'll be busy, bossing everybody in the house around!"

In her room that afternoon, Stephanie pulled out her notebook and started to work on the doll report. It was due tomorrow, and all she could think about was how Wendy, Darcy, and Allie were all mad at her. She was so upset that she felt no satisfaction about getting even with the Flamingoes—well, almost none.

"Dolls," she printed on the top of a clean, empty page. "Dolls are ..." *What?* She had no clue, she thought in growing panic. She had never, ever messed up on a report before.

She had to call Wendy for advice, even if Wendy was still angry. But Wendy was out with Bill Dunlap.

She turned back to her blank page just as her father walked into the room. He wore white overalls and a white painter's cap. His arms were loaded with a can of paint, two big brushes, and a tarp. "Ready to start painting?"

"No!" Stephanie exploded.

"But, honey, I thought you wanted the job done as soon as possible." Danny looked puzzled and a little hurt.

"I do," Stephanie said.

"So what's the problem?"

"Dad, you're doing exactly what *you* want to do." Stephanie blinked back tears.

"Whoa." Danny set everything down and knelt next to Stephanie. "What's going on here?"

"What you want isn't always what I want," Stephanie explained. She tried to stay calm, but her heart pounded like the bass line of a hip-hop song. "You never gave my ideas a chance.

I told you I wanted bright colors—not pink. You're always trying to run my life."

Boy, those words sounded familiar. She remembered why: Wendy had said the same thing to her that afternoon. *Maybe I was trying to run her life. Boss her around, like Darcy and Allie said.*

"Gee, Steph," Danny was saying. "I didn't know you felt that way."

"I tried to tell you what I want," Stephanie told her dad. "Here—look at this." She grabbed *Home Sweet Home* and flipped to a photograph.

Danny studied the page. "Futons, huh?"

Stephanie nodded. "Absolutely, and I love the blue-and-white-striped wallpaper."

Danny nodded. "It does look nice, Steph," he admitted. "And the ceiling hooks would help store stuff that we don't use a lot." He flipped to another page. "And shelves would definitely give you a lot more room."

Danny looked almost convinced, so Stephanie added, "And the futons fold up into couches. That'll give us a *lot* more space in the middle of the room."

Stephanie waited anxiously for her dad's reply. He looked gravely at his daughter. "These ideas are good. Very good," he told her. "I made a big mistake. I guess I didn't listen to you. I was so caught up in what I wanted, I sort of forgot about what you wanted.

"So does that mean I get what I want?"

Danny nodded. "Talk to Michelle. If she agrees, you get what you want."

Stephanie let out a holler. "Yeah!"

Wednesday morning Stephanie walked slowly toward social studies class. She carried three dolls in a plastic bag. She'd had to promise the world to get them from Michelle. But what else could she do? The doll report was due today and she was totally unprepared.

"That was the best connection I've ever seen." Stephanie heard a familiar voice from the middle of the crowded hallway. She turned and saw Wendy surrounded by a group of kids from the Media Club. Wendy whispered something into Bill's ear, and they both burst out laughing.

"Hi, Wendy!" some seventh graders called as they passed by. She grinned and waved at them.

Boy, things sure have changed for Wendy since she stood up to Jenni, Stephanie thought. *She looks so happy, too, not nervous that she'll say the wrong thing. She really does fit in now.*

Then Wendy noticed Stephanie, and the two girls stared at each other. Neither said a word.

Finally Stephanie took a deep breath. "Wendy, I should have listened to you. About me running your life. I know how bad it feels when nobody listens, and, uh, I'm really sorry."

Wendy smiled. "Thanks. Golly, it's nice of you to apologize. You're pretty warm . . . just kidding! You're cool. Very cool."

The two girls grinned. "Oh!" Wendy turned to the group of kids surrounding her. "You remember Bill, right? And this is Erik and Robert and Jean. They're from the Media Club. And guess what?" Wendy beamed. "They want me to join!"

Eric laughed. "We might ask her to be president!" he exclaimed. "She sure knows her way around electronics!"

"Golly, thanks!" Wendy said. "Hey, Steph, first period's our report. Are you ready?"

"Not exactly," Stephanie admitted, showing Wendy the dolls in her plastic bag. "To be honest, I didn't prepare anything. And we never rehearsed together."

"Don't worry," Wendy said reassuringly. "Just talk about how Michelle plays with her dolls. I have the rest of it under control. See you in class."

A few minutes later, as Stephanie settled at her desk, Wendy walked in, lugging three large paper bags.

"The first report will be given by Wendy Gorell and Stephanie Tanner," announced Mr. Cole. "Ready, girls?"

"Definitely!" Wendy hurried to the front of the class.

Oh, no! Stephanie thought nervously, following Wendy. *I'm going to make a total jerk of myself up here. I just know it.*

Wendy began speaking in a clear, confident voice. "Dolls," she said. "You might think they're only for babies. But they can be objects of beauty and art. Some sell for thousands of dollars. But even the ones that don't cost a lot can teach us a lot." She nudged Stephanie.

Stephanie opened her mouth, and out came, "It's very true what Wendy said . . ." She pulled a baby doll with chopped-off hair out of her bag. "They can teach you about . . . hairstyling! In fact, this"—she pointed to the doll's hair—"is my little sister's first effort at combing and styling hair." Everyone giggled. "She's gotten much better since then. These dolls helped my sister understand what a baby was. And how to give love and affection. And that's important . . ." *For what?* Stephanie started to panic. "For every family, especially one as big as mine . . ."

Wendy stepped forward. "Yes, in all families, dolls can be a tradition. My great-grandmother learned how to make dolls when she was a girl living in a mountain cabin. When she had kids of her own, she made dolls for them."

Stephanie held up her second doll. "Modern dolls can have tradition, too," she said quickly. "This one was handed down from my older sister D.J. to me. Now it's my little sister's."

Wendy reached into one of her bags and drew out two large rag dolls. They had embroidered faces, delicate blue glass eyes, and long, flowing hair that looked almost real. Each doll wore a white lace dress with a velvet bow at the collar.

"These are antique dolls, and they are *very* rare," Wendy said proudly. "These dolls are more than seventy years old, but they're still in very good condition. Back then, people couldn't go out and buy a doll. They made them. And it took an awful long time, so they made them to

last. Today dolls are mostly made by machine."
Wendy looked to Stephanie.

Stephanie picked up her third doll. *Whomp!*
The head rolled off and fell to the floor!

The class giggled.

"Uh, as you can see, modern dolls don't last
as long," Stephanie joked, picking the doll's head
off the floor.

Wendy pulled a rag doll with a blank face
out of her second bag. "My great-grandmother
taught my grandmother how to make dolls. She
taught my mom. And my mom is teaching me,"
she said. "I'm still working on this one. And I'm
getting pretty good at making clothes."

She pulled out a tiny red velvet dress and
matching bonnet decorated with fine white lace.
It looked like something a baby princess would
wear.

"Did you design that by yourself?" Renee
Salter asked.

"Yup." Wendy nodded.

"Awesome," another kid said.

Stephanie stared at the dress in amazement.
She had no idea that Wendy was so talented.

Stephanie took a deep breath. "So, from old
to new, you can see that dolls have a special

place in our lives. They're an important part of our culture."

She gave Wendy a questioning look. "That's the end," Wendy announced.

The class applauded and whistled. "Excellent report, girls," Mr. Cole exclaimed. "That's an *A!*"

Wendy and Stephanie turned to each other, faces flushed with happiness. "We did it!" Stephanie whispered as they walked back to their desks. "You were great! Thanks, Wendy. You really saved the report. And my neck!"

Wendy smiled. "You weren't so bad yourself!"

Stephanie spent her lunch period in the library, afraid Darcy and Allie wouldn't talk to her. She had to admit, she couldn't blame them. She had been pretty bossy with Wendy.

But after the final bell Stephanie spotted Darcy and Allie walking away from school. She had to talk to them sometime. "Hey, wait up!" she called.

They stopped and waited silently.

Stephanie shifted uncomfortably from one foot to the other. "Nice dolls Wendy has, huh?" she finally said to break the silence.

"Beautiful," Allie agreed. "I wish I could make clothes like that."

"They were cool. And you know, Wendy's actually kind of cool—in her own way, I mean."

"Especially after she told Jenni off!" Darcy added.

Stephanie grinned. "You know, she is kind of cool. Or, as Wendy would put it, pretty warm."

Silence again. She had to do something! "I'm sorry if I've been a jerk lately," she blurted out. "With the Wendy situation. I wanted to do a great thing. But maybe I went too far."

Darcy threw an arm around Stephanie. "We know you were only trying to help."

"Don't say it! Hurricane Tanner struck again," Stephanie laughed. "And you know, I'm sort of relieved Wendy's got her own friends now. It's hard work, trying to change someone's life."

"Especially when they're a little different," Allie said.

"A little?" Darcy grinned.

"A lot!" Stephanie smiled happily. Things were back to normal with her two best friends!

Danny greeted Stephanie at the door. "I have bad news for you, sweetie," he announced. "D.J.

really wants *her* room painted pink. So I guess we can't use that paint for your room."

Danny tried to keep a straight face, but it didn't work. He broke into a huge grin.

"Let me think about that," Stephanie joked. "Yes! Yes! Yes!"

"Then don't take off your coat," he said. "We've got a lot of shopping to do."

"For bright, striped wallpaper?"

"Well, I don't think—" Danny caught himself and laughed. "Whatever *you* think," he finished.

"Stephanie threw her arms around her dad. "Now you're talking!"

YOU COULD WIN
A VISIT TO THE WARNER BROS. STUDIO!

One First Prize: Trip for up to three people to the Warner Bros. Studios in Burbank, CA, home of the "Full House" Set

Ten Second Prizes: "Stephanie" posters autographed by actress Jodi Sweetin

Twenty-Five Third Prizes: One "Full House" Stephanie Boxed Set

Name_____Birthdate_____

Address_____

City_____State_____Zip_____

Daytime Phone_____

POCKET BOOKS/"Full House" SWEEPSTAKES
Official Rules:

1. No Purchase Necessary. Enter by submitting the completed Official Entry Form (no copies allowed) or by sending on a 3" x 5" card your name, address, daytime telephone number and birthdate to the Pocket Books/"Full House" Sweepstakes, Advertising and Promotion Department, 13th Floor, 1230 Avenue of the Americas, NY, NY 10020. Entries must be received by April 30, 1995. Not responsible for lost, late or misdirected mail. Enter as often as you wish, but one entry per envelope. Winners will be selected at random from all entries received in a drawing to be held on or about May 1, 1995.

2. Prizes: One First Prize: a weekend (3 days/2 nights) for up to three people (the winning minor, his/her parent or legal guardian and one guest) including round-trip coach airfare from the major U.S. airport nearest the winner's residence, ground transportation or car rental, meals and two nights in a hotel (one room, triple occupancy), plus a visit to the Warner Bros. Studios in Burbank, California (approximate retail value: $3,200.00). Winner must be able to travel on the dates designated by sponsor between June 1, 1995 and December 31, 1995. Ten Second Prizes: One "Stephanie" poster autographed by actress Jodi Sweetin (retail value: $15.00) Twenty-Five Third Prizes: One "Full House: Stephanie" Boxed Set (retail value: $14.00).

3. The sweepstakes is open to residents of the U.S. no older than fourteen as of April 30, 1995. Proof of age required to claim prize. Prizes will be awarded to the winner's parent or legal guardian. Void in Puerto Rico and wherever else prohibited by law. Employees of Paramount Communications, Inc., Warner Bros., their suppliers, affiliates, agencies, participating retailers, and their families living in the same household are not eligible. One prize per person or household. Prizes are not transferable and may not be substituted. The odds of winning a prize depend upon the number of entries received.

4. All federal, state and local taxes are the responsibility of the winners. Winners will be notified by mail. Prize winners may be required to execute and return an Affidavit of Eligibility and Release within 15 days of notification or an alternate winner will be selected. Winners grant Pocket Books and Warner Bros. the right to use their names, likenesses, and entries for any advertising, promotion and publicity purposes without further compensation to or permission from the entrants, except where prohibited by law. For a list of major prize winners, (available after May 5, 1995) send a stamped, self-addressed envelope to Prize Winners, Pocket Books/"Full House: Stephanie" Sweepstakes, Advertising and Promotion Department, 13th Floor, 1230 Avenue of the Americas, NY, NY 10020.

FULL HOUSE, characters, names and all related indicia are trademarks of Warner Bros. Television © 1994.

Oct94-01